A DARK DAWN IN TEXAS

On her deathbed in the spring of 1875, Laura Peters shocks her son Paul by belatedly revealing that his uncle did not die alongside his father in the bloody confrontation at Gettysburg twelve years before. She urges Paul to ride west in a quest to find this relative who holds a guilty secret from those dreadful Civil War days. With mixed emotions he takes up the challenge, eventually arriving in the Texas town of Ongar Ridge — only to find himself accused of murdering the man he has been seeking . . .

Books by Richard Smith
in the Linford Western Library:

REVENGE FOR A HANGING
MEXICAN MERCY MISSION

RICHARD SMITH

A DARK DAWN IN TEXAS

Complete and Unabridged

LINFORD
Leicester

First published in Great Britain in 2017 by
Robert Hale
an imprint of The Crowood Press
Wiltshire

First Linford Edition
published 2020
by arrangement with
The Crowood Press
Wiltshire

A catalogue record for this book is available
from the British Library.

ISBN 978–1–4448–4536–5

Published by
Ulverscroft Limited
Anstey, Leicestershire

Set by Words & Graphics Ltd.
Anstey, Leicestershire
Printed and bound in Great Britain by
T. J. International Ltd., Padstow, Cornwall

1

In the spring of 1875 Laura Peters knew she was close to death. Her breathing was shallow and her body was racked with constant pain.

Life had been hard for the widow who, with a little help from neighbours, had struggled to survive with her son Paul during the war and its aftermath following Lee's surrender at Appomattox Court House. Their horses had been requisitioned during the war, but their property — unlike many others — had been left intact. From an early age Paul had worked at a physical level way beyond what could be reasonably expected for his years as he helped his exhausted mother survive by cultivating crops and looking after those few chickens and goats left to them by hungry soldiers.

Despite their struggles Laura somehow managed to make time to educate her son. She herself came from educated parents, and she used her own literary and mathematical talents to ensure that Paul would be equipped for a life that could extend beyond simple farm work.

Now she decided that it was time to make a request which, if he accepted, would take him far away from his homeland.

'Paul, I've got something to ask you.'

'Yes, Ma. I hate to see you so unwell. You know I'll do anything to help. What is it?'

'It's nothing to do with my health, son. It's a challenge you can accept or ignore. It's your choice, but I realize that you may not wish to stay here after I'm gone and there's something important you should know about your family.'

Paul was intrigued but mystified. 'My family? You're my family. My only family. What do you mean?'

'I mean that you needn't be alone if you choose to go in search of your uncle.'

'My uncle? You mean Uncle Jack?'

Fearing that his mother's ill health was impacting on her reasoning, Paul took her hand in his and gently pointed out that his uncle, along with his father, had died at Gettysburg.

'No,' whispered his mother. 'I believe he is still alive, though living far away from us.'

As she spoke, Laura pulled out a crumpled letter she had held under her pillow. 'He wrote to me,' she said. 'But I've been reluctant — scared, I suppose — to show it to you before. Now I think it's time.'

Slowly, disbelievingly, Paul took the paper from his mother's trembling hand. It was dated 3 July 1868.

My dear Laura
This is a most difficult letter to write, and I hope it does not shock you too much. I trust that you were

told officially that my brother Bruce died at Gettysburg, and I guess that you were also told, or you at least assumed, that I was dead too — even if the official word might have been that I was listed as missing.

In fact, I have to tell you that I am living under an assumed name on the other side of the Mississippi, many miles away from my beloved Virginia and from you and my nephew Paul. I think of you and pray for you every day. To my great shame, I could not return to you after the hostilities, and believe I cannot do so in safety even now. I cannot reveal too much detail without putting myself in danger because of an act which troubles my soul every single day and night.

I pray that you are both well, though I know you must have suffered greatly during the terrible years since your husband and I rode away on what we thought was a just and noble mission. None of us could have imagined the horrors that were to follow and the thousands who were to suffer death, injury or deprivation. I am desperate to tell you that your husband fought bravely and honourably and was a credit to us. If it is any comfort to you after all this time, you should know that he died in my arms after being badly wounded in the heat of battle.

Selfishly, I am wary of writing more, since this letter could fall into the wrong hands. I can only say that I am now striving to atone for my guilty past by using the rest of my life to good effect. I only wish that I could share it with you, since you should know that I dearly love you both.

Please destroy this letter when you have read it, but know that you and Paul are always in my thoughts.

The letter was unsigned, though it was obvious who had sent it. And of course, it had not been destroyed. It had lain hidden among Laura's possessions until she handed it to Paul, nearly seven years after it had been written.

Now he hugged his mother, with mixed feelings of joy and anger. For all these long years he had been told that the two brothers had died in battle. Now he knew that to be a monstrous lie, and that one of them, his uncle, had survived.

'Mother, why didn't you tell me earlier?'

'Because, my son, I was a coward. I was in shock for days. Then I was scared how you would react if I showed you the letter. You were too young to take any action. Now I want you to decide whether you want to ignore it, or perhaps even see if you can find the man who meant so much to your father and to me. Maybe you can help him come to terms with whatever is this guilt which he doesn't explain.'

Laura paused, breathless, allowing Paul to ask what she would want him to say to his uncle if he were ever to see him.

'Tell him I despise him for not coming back to us when we were in so much need. Whatever his crime was, he should have faced up to it and sought forgiveness here rather than many miles away. More than that, though, you should tell him that I never stopped loving him. I loved them both — your father and your uncle. It gave me great happiness to learn from this letter that one of them still lived, when for years I had grieved for two goodly men who had meant so much to me. Whatever his sin, I found consolation knowing that your Uncle Jack was with your father when he met his Maker. I'd like him to know that.'

*   *   *

Touched by his mother's devotion to both men, Paul Peters made the momentous decision that he would indeed seek to find her missing brother-in-law. Whatever the mysterious truth that was half revealed in the letter, he desperately wanted to meet his only surviving relative.

After Laura's funeral, he handed over their land and possessions to the care of a neighbour and set off on a quest that was to last nearly three years as he rode further west trying to find any trace of Jack Peters. When he rode into the Texas town of Ongar Ridge late at night in July 1878, he was confident that he had at last located the man he had sought for so long.

Utterly exhausted, it was the greatest of cruel ironies that he made the decision to check straight into one of the town's hotels and leave meeting his uncle until the following morning. It was a decision he was to regret deeply, as it had many repercussions.

2

Mike Rowland was just starting his usual morning round of Ongar Ridge's main street when young Jake Thornton came running up behind him.

'Marshal, turn round and come with me. Quick. Come to Mr Jackson's print shop.'

The boy was considerably agitated, so the town marshal took his request seriously and turned back towards the converted barn that was used for the production of the weekly *Ongar Tribune*. With Jake pressing him to hurry, he did indeed quicken his normally measured pace when he saw that a poster-sized sheet had been pinned over the notice board fixed outside the ramshackle building. It usually displayed the week's main news item. The replacement notice, however, now carried the single word

9

JUSTICE in large print.

The door to the barn was gaping open and the marshal followed the boy's excited admonitions to go inside. Immediately the marshal realized that he was treading on a mess of metal type which had been tipped haphazardly over the floor. He stepped further into the building and saw more devastation. Racks of newsprint and other materials had been upturned, and back copies of the newspaper had been pulled from the wooden racks on which they had been carefully stored.

Worst of all, though, was the sight of Peter Jackson, the editor of the *Tribune*. His dead body was slumped in a corner and it was clear, even in the gloom, that he carried a vicious stab wound in his stomach. Sticking out from the bloody mess was a huge Bowie knife which was stabbed through another printed notice, again carrying the single word JUSTICE.

The picture before the marshal was made even more horrific by the fact that printers' ink had been tipped over Jackson's body to run down and mingle with his congealing blood. The ink's half-empty container remained by his side.

Marshal Rowland did not need to be a master detective to come quickly to a number of conclusions. First, it was obvious that someone had known of Jackson's routine. Every Friday night he finished the task of getting his week's news content into type and prepared for printing early on Saturday morning so that it was ready for distribution by young Jake Thornton and two of his friends. It was a timetable designed to ensure that, before the first Sunday church service, everyone would know the news and would have a ready store of information and gossip to enliven their discourse.

The other obvious fact was that Jackson's killer had been familiar enough with the type setting and printing process to know how to select and order the metal so that it would print properly. This narrowed the list of possible suspects to some degree but Mike Rowland remembered how Jackson had always been more than happy to show visitors, of whatever age, how the reverse type was used to give a correct image when printed. During the years Jackson had run his print shop, many customers had watched as he prepared notices and other literature for them. Furthermore, the marshal recognized that, despite the variable levels of literacy which existed amongst the area's citizens, many of those who had visited the print shop were quite capable of correctly spelling the single printed word which had been used to send some sort of message to the authorities and the general public.

But what was its significance? Justice, or revenge, for what crime?

'Close the door and don't let anyone inside until I get back,' the marshal told eight-year-old Jake. 'I'm trusting you to guard things while I'm gone.'

He started to leave but then turned

back to the youngster. 'Well done for coming and finding me. I think you can expect a reward to make up for losing your newspaper delivery pay.'

'Thanks, Marshal, but where you goin'?'

'To get some witnesses. Won't be long.'

* * *

Still puzzling over the morning's shocking event, Marshal Rowland decided that there was little point in immediately calling in the town's only doctor. There was nothing a medical man could do for Peter Jackson, and the cause of death was obvious. Instead the lawman returned to his office where he picked up his deputy, Luke Granger. He briefly explained what had happened before he sent Luke off to alert the undertaker, Jasper Ryan, that his services would be needed.

'I'm going to get Eustace Trimble,' he

told his deputy. 'I want you to meet me back at the newspaper office to act as a witness to the scene before we get the doc to look at him and then get Jasper to deal with the body.'

Now aged forty-six, Marshal Mike Rowland carried his years well. His body was lean and muscular, and the only signs of ageing were skin creases round his eyes and the beginning of grey in his hair — though this was barely known since he was rarely seen without a hat. He had become the town's marshal after he had found himself unemployed when the Texas Rangers were temporarily disbanded by the victorious authorities after the war between the northern and southern states. After earlier years fighting Comanche and seeing action in the Mexican War of 1856-58, he found himself at a loss when his Texas Rangers' life came to an end.

Unlike many of his companions, he did not join the Confederate forces during the war. He felt that it was no concern of his and that a regimented army life was no substitute for his more independent action as a Ranger.

With no domestic or romantic ties, he had ridden around Texas and Arizona Territory somewhat aimlessly before arriving at Ongar Ridge. Drinking one evening in the Golden Bullet Saloon, he had intervened to stop a fight between two drunks from turning into something more serious. The town's elderly marshal had been too slow to reach the scene, so Mike Rowland had pushed himself between the two men who were arguing over some kind of bet, and with a single punch knocked one of them to the ground before turning back to the other burly figure and twisting his arm behind his back until he quietened down. It was all done with a simple efficiency which greatly impressed all those observing the few seconds of calm action.

Within days of this incident, the town's sixty-five-year-old marshal faced up to the citizens' general dissatisfaction with his performance and declared his intention to retire. Two weeks later the town's council offered the job to Rowland. 'We all liked the efficient way you dealt with that brawl without resorting to any weapon,' the mayor told him.

'I can shoot if need be,' had been the laconic reply before Rowland, whose funds were running perilously low, agreed to be sworn in at a salary not much above the miserly pay he had been getting as a Texas Ranger.

Now, eleven years later, he got the mayor out of bed to tell him that their newspaper editor had been killed. A short, plump man with an inflated view of his own importance, Eustace Trimble was none too pleased to be woken by the marshal's insistent hammering at his door. Eventually it was opened by the live-in housekeeper, who relayed Mike Rowland's message that the mayor was to come and attend to some important business.

The marshal fumed when he was kept waiting nearly twenty minutes before Trimble appeared, wearing the dark city clothes he had adopted since his election to the town's highest office. The man had originally come south from Chicago and had made himself comparatively wealthy by overcharging for the variety of goods he sold in his general store. With no serious competition within miles, he had little difficulty adding a very respectable profit margin to goods ordered from his contacts back in Chicago and elsewhere.

When he stood for election he had garnered support by offering special deals to those who — truthfully or not — promised to cast their votes in his favour.

Now, breathing heavily, he scurried behind the marshal as they made their way to the newspaper office and workshop. Despite the relatively early hour, a small crowd had already gathered. The news had been spread by young Jake's two contemporaries when they had arrived to start their delivery

17

chores but were informed that their employer was no longer in a position to appreciate their weekly endeavours.

Despite his tender years, Jake Thornton had done a valiant job of guarding the print shop entrance until the deputy marshal, Luke Granger, arrived to assume control. Now Luke followed his boss and a red-faced Eustace Trimble into the print shop to view the evidence of Peter Jackson's untimely death.

When they reappeared the crowd outside had swollen to around thirty people. 'Who did it?' yelled a female voice when Mike Rowland confirmed that the editor was dead, and that it wasn't from natural causes.

'Reckon I know.' The assertion came in the rough voice of a male shouting unnecessarily loudly from the side of the compact gathering that was pressing towards the marshal. 'There's a young fella new in town. Saw him coming out of the hotel and going to Mr Choo's eating house.'

The information came from Red

Roberts, one of three brothers who, over the past six years, had consistently given Marshal Rowland trouble. 'C'mon, Marshal, let's go get 'im. He needs stringing up for what he done.'

Sensing a degree of support for the suggestion of immediate retribution, Mike Rowland held his hand in the air to seek silence from the steadily growing crowd. 'We'll have no more talk of that kind, Red Roberts. Let's all calm down. If this man is involved, we'll deal with him in a proper legal manner. Anyone know where he is now?'

An excited female voice piped up. 'Still in Mr Choo's, I reckon. Tall young man with a black hat,' said Frau Kruger, one of the town's many European immigrants.

'Yep, that's him,' shouted Roberts. 'Let's go get him.'

'Told you to calm down,' ordered the marshal. 'You stay out of it.' He turned to his deputy. 'Luke, you come with me and we'll see what the fella has got to say for himself.'

* ★ *

When the two men entered the eating house, they kept their guns holstered but quickly spread themselves wide, so as to present a dispersed target if there should be any trouble. Their quarry was immediately identifiable as there were only five customers seated at Mr Choo's polished wooden tables. Two were known ranch hands; two were travelling drummers who had been in town trying to sell their wares for the last three days; and — seated alone with his back to the far wall — was a stranger fitting the description the marshal had been given. He looked up from his meal at the two law officers now intently scrutinizing him.

'Looking for someone, Marshal?' he asked in a quietly controlled voice carrying an accent which placed him as coming from further east. Having posed his question, he continued forking his breakfast from his plate to his mouth, giving the impression of being neither concerned nor alarmed at being the centre of attention.

'Yep. I'd like a few words with you, Mister,' said the marshal. 'First, what's your name, and what's your business in our town?'

As Mike Rowland asked his question, tiny Mr Choo shuffled through from the cooking area with a full plate in each hand. The Chinaman stopped abruptly as he took in the scene before him and let out a squeaky little scream of alarm.

'No need to concern yourself, my friend,' the marshal assured him 'There won't be any trouble, will there be, Mr . . .'

As the last part of his comment was obviously addressed to the seated man, the stranger stopped eating and replied to the marshal's questions.

'There won't be trouble from me, Marshal, and you'll find I signed my name when I registered at the hotel last night. It's Peters, Paul Peters. Now, what's this all about? Can't a man eat

21

his breakfast in peace in this town? You coming in here like this don't seem to be a very friendly welcoming committee. Now can I finish my meal?'

'Sure you can, but you won't mind if I sit down with you and drink a coffee. Then I'd like you to come and answer a few questions in my office.'

* * *

When the three men left Mr Choo's place ten minutes later, Red Roberts was waiting outside. 'Glad to see you got him, Marshal. If we ain't gonna string him up, make sure you lock him up safe. We don't want a murderer runnin' around loose.' As he spoke, Roberts moved aggressively towards the stranger, as if ready to strike him. He stopped abruptly, however, and rapidly took a step backwards in sudden alarm when he saw that the man in front of him was holding a Colt .45 pointed at his chest — a weapon that seemed to have come from nowhere in a fraction of a second.

Though daunted, Roberts added to his bluster by spitting at the stranger's feet, but still kept a careful eye on the pistol pointing at him.

The stranger stood motionless but ignored the taunt with a look which appeared to be one of contempt rather than concern. The man holding the gun turned to the marshal. 'Guess you better get this hothead out of my sight pretty damn quick before I do something we might all regret.'

Initially taken by surprise, the marshal recovered quickly and addressed Roberts in a tone designed to brook no dissent. 'Do as the man says, Red, and make yourself scarce. I'm dealing with this and I don't want trouble from you.'

Glowering, Roberts wisely did as he had been told, as the marshal turned his attention back to the stranger. 'Perhaps you had better let me take care of that weapon, Mister,' he said, and was pleasantly surprised at the

23

readiness with which the stranger complied.

3

After the arrest Marshal Rowland kept Paul Peters in jail for three weeks until the circuit judge arrived for the trial. The stranger was accused of the murder of Peter Jackson, the editor of the *Ongar Tribune*. During that time the prisoner had steadfastly refused to give more information than his name and a flat denial that he knew anything about the death of the stabbed newspaperman.

Public sentiment in Ongar Ridge was mixed. On their frequent visits to the town, the three Roberts brothers had consistently been heard asserting that the stranger, Paul Peters, was obviously the culprit. Who else could it have been, they asked those drinking with them in the Golden Bullet. Most agreed with them that it couldn't be a coincidence that Jackson had been found dead within hours of the stranger arriving. And there were many townsfolk who, although normally holding the Roberts trio in low esteem, were persuaded by the strength of what seemed to be logical assertions from the brothers. Their accusation seemed to make sense.

Other citizens, though, were more prepared to reserve judgement pending the upcoming trial.

The prisoner himself did nothing to divert attention away from himself as the prime suspect. When his meagre prison rations were delivered, he received them politely but refused to respond to any personal questions about his background or his reasons for being in Ongar Ridge.

Deputy Marshal Luke Granger was particularly inclined to add to the general consensus that the man in jail must have something to hide. 'Damn fella don't say nothin'. Just repeats that he don't know a thing about a murder. Guess he'll have to say something at his trial, though,' Granger told anyone he talked to.

The mystery of the editor's death, and the fact that there seemed to be only one suspect, meant that there was a good attendance when the circuit judge called the proceedings to a start in the town's small courthouse. It was a sign of Ongar Ridge's initial civic confidence that the building had been erected early on in the town's existence. Lawlessness was a real problem in the aftermath of the prolonged war between the North and the South, and resources were scarce as the defeated southerners lived through what was called the Period of Reconstruction. Nevertheless, a couple of cattlemen who had gained capital from supplying livestock to the north were confident that their Texas town would flourish, as westward expansion looked certain to continue. Buoyed up by these beliefs they had been prepared to invest for growth.

They were determined, however, that their town would escape the worst excesses of a period of economic hardship with its resulting banditry and violence. So, alongside a couple of hotels and saloons, their construction priorities were a church, a marshal's office with two cells, and a small courthouse capable of being extended if necessary.

Despite their intentions, the courthouse had never actually been enlarged, though it had hosted numerous trials, varying from neighbourhood disputes to horse theft and murder. Now, at the opening of the stranger's murder trial, it was full to overflowing with a mixture of people who felt a genuine connexion with the dead editor, or had nothing better to do with their time.

Curiosity was a big factor, too, especially amongst the town's women. Still outnumbered by the male population, the womenfolk had no need to worry themselves about a lack of potential partners, despite the deaths of those who had left to fight in the war. This new arrival had created more than usual interest, however, since the relatively small number of female citizens who had clapped eyes on the young stranger had gossiped that he was particularly good looking.

The trial, therefore, afforded a chance for both sexes to get a good look at the tall, handsome newcomer who confirmed his name and pronounced himself not guilty in an educated Virginian accent.

The jury members sworn in by Judge Joseph Kane were a mixed bunch, but included a couple of homesteaders who had been persuaded by the three Roberts brothers that the trial result was a foregone conclusion and that a speedy guilty verdict would let them get back to their crops and livestock within a few days.

Judge Kane seemed equally keen to bring matters to a speedy conclusion. A thin, angular man with a crop of unruly hair, his clipped speech was delivered in a loud manner which demanded attention, and indicated his authority. His gout had been particularly troublesome for a couple of weeks and he was clearly not inclined to let proceedings last longer than necessary, especially as he was anxious to get back to Austin in time for his daughter's wedding. He didn't much care for Jennifer's choice of beau, and was determined to warn her young man that there would be dire consequences if he didn't meet the standards his future father-in-law expected for the bride's happiness and general well-being.

The judge listened intently as the middle-aged and distinguished prosecution lawyer called on Marshal Rowland to describe the scene he had faced in the print shop, and to make the obvious statement that the Bowie knife wound in Peter Jackson's body had been the cause of death. He also described the JUSTICE posters.

This descriptive evidence was confirmed by the deputy marshal, who was sternly admonished by the judge when he pointed at the defendant, Paul

Peters, whilst describing what he termed 'the killer's vicious attack on poor Mr Jackson'.

Next, the prosecutor called on the town's mayor, Eustace Trimble, to give evidence. With his usual self-important manner, Trimble began by telling how he had been woken by the marshal and had then accompanied him to the workshop barn to survey the murder scene. He was soon interrupted by the impatient judge, however. 'Are you just going to repeat what we have already heard from two other witnesses?' he demanded. The mayor blanched before admitting that he had nothing to add, except to state the town's respect for the deceased. Trimble was curtly told he could stand down from the witness box.

The judge then challenged Charles Fisher, the prosecuting attorney, to produce any witnesses he had who might shed light on the actual killing, or information about the significance of the two printed notices which might give a clue to a murderer's motives. Fisher quietly admitted that there was nothing.

Impatient to press on, Judge Kane invited the young and rather nervous lawyer defending Paul Peters to make a preliminary statement. Speaking without much conviction, he said that he had consulted with the accused, who had nothing to say except that he was amazed he had been held on any charges, and that there was nothing whatsoever to link him to the death of the newspaper editor. He had reiterated that he was not guilty. The lawyer called one surprise witness for the defence, however. The clerk at the Presido Hotel where Paul Peters had stayed on the night he arrived in Ongar Ridge swore on oath that the accused man had not come down from his room until after eight o'clock, which was some while after Peter Jackson's body had been discovered by young Jake Thornton.

When challenged, the clerk was adamant that he had been at his desk in the lobby all night. He had checked in the exhausted stranger not long before midnight, and he was certain the man had not left his room until he came down after eight and asked where he could get a decent breakfast. 'I sent him to the Chinaman's, of course,' added the clerk, as if that somehow confirmed there could be no doubt about the veracity of his account.

This extra evidence served to throw some doubt into the minds of those sitting or standing in the crowded court. There was suddenly a burst of noise as people turned to those next to them to question what had previously seemed to be a clear certainty. Perhaps the stranger was not the killer after all.

Judge Kane was quick to silence the questioning chatter. With obvious anger, he banged his gavel loudly on the counter before him. 'Silence in court,' he demanded, before turning to address the jury. 'This trial is a farce, and I am stopping it now. There is not a shred of evidence to link the accused man with the editor's death. The jury is dismissed and you, Paul Peters, are free to go. These proceedings are closed, so clear the court.'

Reluctantly, those present started to leave the building. Many felt cheated by the way things had turned out. The whole hearing had taken less than two hours and fair-minded citizens realized that they were no nearer to knowing why their editor, Peter Jackson, had died. Some had less open minds, however. As the court emptied, Red Roberts could be heard shouting his views. 'I still reckon he did it. Guilty as hell, I reckon.'

★ ★ ★

After the court had been cleared of all observers, Marshal Rowland approached Paul Peters, who had remained standing by the judge's bench. 'What happens now, fella?' he asked. 'A lot of people are not going to believe you had nothing to do with

34

the killing, despite what the judge says. I don't reckon it's a good idea for you to stay in Ongar Ridge. Some folk might not take kindly to the idea that a maybe killer is walking around their town. Clearly some will think you've got away with murdering an innocent man, without being punished for it. Where you going to right now, fella? I suggest you make yourself real scarce.'

'Right now, Marshal, I'm going back to the hotel, and after that you'll still see me around. Sorry to disappoint you but I've got business to settle and I'm not leaving until I've done it.'

Concerned that his advice was clearly going to be ignored, Marshal Rowland decided to try to get more in tune with the stranger's intentions and his reasons for wanting to stay in Ongar Ridge. Paul Peters had been judged to be not guilty of any crime and had caused no trouble whilst held in his cell before the trial. There was no valid reason for the marshal to regard him with undue suspicion, but he was worried that the man's presence somehow constituted a threat to the maintenance of law and order. Peters had already demonstrated a calm coolness, and an ability to defend himself if necessary, and the marshal judged him to be a man who would not back away from trouble.

'Whatever your business, perhaps I can help?' the lawman volunteered without expecting anything too positive to result from his query. He was therefore somewhat surprised by the firmly stated response.

'You need to believe, Marshal, that I did not kill Peter Jackson and I've got my own reasons for finding out who did. I intend to do whatever it takes to reveal the killer, so I hope we two are on the same side.' Paul Peters paused, waiting to see how Marshal Rowland would respond. Could he count on assistance from the lawman who, just a few minutes earlier, had indicated that he wished him out of the way?

There was a long silence whilst the marshal considered his response. All the time the stranger had been held in prison he had been uncommunicative. Now he seemed to have changed his stance and was apparently looking for some kind of partnership to help him in his self-appointed task of discovering who had killed the editor. He seemed to be genuine in his desire and the marshal decided it was better to side with the stranger's apparently good intentions, rather than regard his involvement as a possible hindrance in the quest to find the culprit.

'OK, Mr Peters. It sounds as if we are on the same side. But I need you to tell me what your interest is. What are the personal reasons you mentioned?'

'The most personal reason possible, Marshal. I'm certain Peter Jackson is — was — my uncle, my pa's brother. So you'll see I really am concerned to get justice for him.'

'Your father's brother? But how can that be? You've told me your surname is Peters. His was Jackson. It doesn't add up.'

'Actually it does, Marshal. You see, I'm certain that his real name was Jack Peters. I think that when he ran away from his past he reversed his name and turned Jack Peters into Peter Jackson, which was what you all knew him as.'

Marshal Rowland strode purposefully up the central aisle of the emptied court house while he took in this bit of information. He had to decide whether he accepted what he had just been told and, if so, what he was going to do about it. He turned and walked slowly back to the man called Peters, who was claiming to be the nephew of the respected newspaperman.

'I think I need some proof. Tell me, for instance, what the murdered man looked like.'

'Marshal, I can't do that. I haven't set eyes on him since I was no bigger than knee height. I've no idea what he might have looked like now.'

'That's not very helpful, Peters. What about any special features you can recall?'

'No, I can't describe what he looked like now — but there is something. A couple of weeks before he rode off to the war, he had a bit of an accident. Although I was very young I remember it because it was the first time I'd seen blood. He was fooling around with one of our dogs when the animal bit off one of his fingers — the smallest one. Think it was his left hand. Reckon that might have stayed the same after all these years. Did the editor have that?'

'Yep, he did, so it sounds like he was your man. OK But if I swallow your story, you had better tell me why you say he would have taken on a false identity.'

'Sorry, Marshal, but I can't do that. Not yet, anyway, because I only know a bit of the story myself. That's why I came to Ongar Ridge. I wanted to meet my uncle, who I had long believed had died in the war. I came to hear his story, which he had only hinted at in a letter to my mother. That's why I need your help to fill in the picture. Perhaps together we can find out what's behind this JUSTICE business, and therefore who it was knifed my uncle. Is it a deal?'

Marshal Rowland's mind was made up. He stuck out his hand. 'Yep. Guess so. Shake on it. But there's one more thing. What are you going to do if you somehow find out who killed Peter Jackson? I noticed you were pretty handy with that Colt. Hope you don't have ideas of carrying out retribution yourself!'

'No, Marshal. I don't count myself as a law breaker. I'd like to think I would hand it over to you to make sure that the killer ended up with rope around his neck. You're the man wearing the badge, and I respect that.'

4

Committed to aiding Paul Peters in his efforts to trace his uncle's killer in Ongar Ridge, Marshal Rowland suggested two sources where he might seek information.

'I think you might usefully start with our most experienced lawyer, Charles Fisher.'

'I know the name, Marshal. Wasn't he the one who set out the case against me at the trial?'

'That's right. But don't hold that against him. He's a good man, and I know he was quite friendly with your uncle. In fact, he was involved in helping him set up the newspaper business when he first arrived in Ongar Ridge. Your uncle took over a rather rundown operation that had been left unused when the previous owner of the print shop died from a heart attack. The man had no kin and the place was just left empty. Don't know the details, but somehow Charles Fisher arranged that your uncle could take it over.'

'Thanks, Marshal. Anyone else I should see?'

'I suggest Bessie Pullman. Your uncle lodged with her. But be sensitive how you handle it. Everyone took it as read that there was something a lot closer than that in their relationship. She was certainly very cut up at the funeral. Shed buckets of tears.'

'Yep. The funeral you wouldn't let me attend — though I guess I understand why,' said Peters with a wry expression on his sun-bronzed face. 'Guess folk wouldn't have understood why the prisoner suspected of the murder should be allowed to be present at the burial. Might have been different if they knew he was my close relative. But I still want to keep that secret, Marshal. Think it might be easier to seek answers if the relationship is kept under wraps, at least for now.'

'OK. If that's the way you want to play it, I'll keep it under my hat.'

* * *

Mike Rowland's advice turned out to be sound. Lawyer Charles Fisher was indeed a valuable source of information. He told the story of how the man he knew as Peter Jackson had arrived in Ongar Ridge with little money but a wish to settle in a community where he could start a new life after the horrors of the bloody civil war which had set states against states, conflicting ideologies against each other, and — in extreme cases — even brother against brother.

'He didn't say much at all about his own background or experiences. To tell the truth, I rather suspected that he had been a deserter. But he was certainly excited as hell when I mentioned the printing business standing derelict. I held some paperwork which let me give him the go-ahead to take it over. I even lent him some of my own money to buy supplies to get it going. He soon taught himself the mechanics involved in the jobbing print trade, and within a few months he was able to launch the *Ongar Tribune*. Right from the start he used it to be outspoken about matters he thought needed exposing. It seemed like he was determined to be some kind of avenging angel, but using ink rather than bullets as his weapon.'

The lawyer paused to draw on his cheroot, paced round his well-appointed office, then stood with his back to the window which looked out over Ongar Ridge's rutted main street.

'Made himself a few enemies,' he continued. 'But he won a lot of plaudits, too. Decent folk appreciated his often brave stance against what he perceived to be wrong doing. In the end, though, our esteemed editor must have gone too far. It would seem that someone obviously took strong offence at his worthy campaigning and decided to end it with a killing.'

'Any idea who that might be, Mr Fisher?'

The lawyer stubbed out the remains of his cheroot. 'Now that really is a leading question, young man, and one you can hardly expect me to answer. But I can offer a suggestion, if you see it as your business.'

'Mr Fisher, I think I have a legitimate reason to concern myself. After all, I was accused of murder, wasn't I? Perhaps folk won't be surprised if I make it my business to try to clear my name by exposing the person who killed Peter Jackson. So what's your suggestion?'

'It's quite simple, really. I'm sure there are back copies of all the old *Tribune* issues in the print shop. I guess I'm the owner now, so you have my permission to help yourself to whatever you can find in there.'

'Thank you. I appreciate it.' Peters paused for a minute. 'Perhaps I could go a bit further than that. How about I tidy the whole place up, and even think about starting up some kind of news-sheet myself? Not as grand or professional as the *Tribune*, perhaps, but something to justify my continued stay in Ongar Ridge and even earn a bit of money.'

The idea obviously chimed with the lawyer. 'You're welcome, son. There's a couple of young lads who would be happy to help you, I'm sure. Jake Thornton and his pals used to assist with deliveries and even a bit of printing, so I'm sure you could get them in to help clear up and get things rolling. Oh, and there's also Bessie Pullman. She used to help with some of the typesetting. Might be worth contacting her.'

'Thanks. She was already on my list. I'll have a word with her.'

* * *

Bessie Pullman lived in a neat, white-painted clapperboard house on the outskirts of the town, just opposite the print shop barn. Its style was very much like many of those on the eastern seaboard, which was not at all surprising for that is where she and her husband had originally come from. They had intended heading for California but finally settled in Texas when, weary of travelling, Greg Pullman decided it was as good a place as any to establish himself in his trade as a baker, initially serving the hopeful prospectors who had heard that silver had been discovered in the area but who were mostly sadly disillusioned when their endeavours produced few results.

Since Pullman's death from pleurisy in 1872, his widow had continued the bakery business with the help of a younger married woman, whose husband, William Shackleton, was the town's blacksmith. It was a bad marriage, however, since he spent most of his earnings, and much of his time, playing poker in the Golden Bullet. His wife, Jessica, had suffered two miscarriages and the doc had expressed the opinion that she was almost certainly not capable of having children. This news had deeply upset William and he had increasingly ignored her, and also increased his drinking.

He had not dissented when Bessie Pullman offered Jessica an early morning job in the bakery. In practice he was hardly aware of his wife's absence, since she was home in time to have a breakfast ready for him when he roused himself late after returning from the saloon well after midnight. His habits were well known and his customers knew there was little point seeking his services before late morning.

⋆ ⋆ ⋆

At first Mrs Pullman was somewhat hostile when Paul Peters knocked at her door and introduced himself.

'Sure, I know who you are,' she acknowledged. 'You're the stranger accused of killing Peter Jackson in his print shop. I went to your trial.'

'Yes, Ma'am — accused, but not guilty. I didn't do it and I'm as anxious as anyone to find out who did.'

'Why should you care? If you say it wasn't you, then what does it matter to you who killed him?'

'Well, Ma'am, let's just say I'm anxious to clear my name, but there is another thing. I've been told what a force for good Mr Jackson was with the *Ongar Tribune* and I have thoughts of perhaps being able to continue with his work. I understand that he had a lodging room with you, Ma'am, and you probably knew him better than anyone else. I was hoping, Ma'am, that you might be kind enough to spare some time to tell me about him, and perhaps even confidentially give me any thoughts you might have on who would have wanted him dead.'

Bessie Pullman suddenly softened her attitude, perhaps persuaded that the young man was sincere in his good intentions and might indeed make a valuable replacement for the dead editor.

'I was about to eat when you arrived,' she said. 'Would you like to share a meal with me while I tell you what I can about Peter? He was a complex man.'

A pleasantly rounded woman, with rosy cheeks and her fair hair tied back in a style that suited her still youthful appearance, Bessie Pullman served up a steaming beef stew accompanied by the crisp bread rolls that brought many satisfied customers back to her bakery on a regular basis.

As they ate, she readily started telling her visitor about her long-term connection with the man she knew as Peter Jackson. Feeling guilty at the deception, Paul Peters was tempted to tell her that this was an alias, and to reveal that the dead editor was actually his own uncle. However, he decided that, as a naturally talkative person, Bessie Pullman would probably find it impossible to keep that information secret as she chatted to her customers. At least for the time being, he decided to keep that knowledge restricted to the town's marshal, who had agreed to respect his request for confidentiality.

'Mr Jackson started lodging with me and my husband soon after he arrived in Ongar Ridge,' said Bessie Pullman. 'It was much cheaper for him than staying in the hotel, and it was useful extra income for us. He was extremely helpful when my husband became ill, and that allowed me to keep the bakery going when Greg could no longer manage.'

'Ma'am, you said earlier that Mr Jackson was a complex man. What did you mean by that?'

Mrs Pullman pondered a few moments before answering. 'Well, as I said, he was always helpful to most folk and seemed generally satisfied with his work reporting on events in the town and elsewhere, but he could be really antagonistic if he thought someone was doing wrong or something unlawful. It was a favourite saying of his that sins should not go unpunished. He was almost like a preacher when he got going. Although he was Christian in his general attitude, he was never one for forgiveness, even if he was reporting something like a minor theft.'

After their meal, Bessie Pullman continued to talk about her own life before she and her husband had come west. 'I've sometimes been tempted to go back east,' she said, 'but Peter was a good companion after my Greg died. I don't know what I'll do now that he's gone too.'

Her listener noticed a catch in her voice, as she surreptitiously wiped a tear from her eye, leaving Paul Peters convinced that the editor's death constituted far more than the loss of a lodger. He formed the firm opinion that the widow could be a committed ally in his quest to solve the mystery of his uncle's stabbing, and asked that she use her contacts with bakery customers to spread the news that he was intending to stick around and had thoughts of reviving the newspaper.

He had not formed any clear idea of what he was going to do, but felt some kind of imperative desire to investigate the history of the editor who had been his only surviving relative until his untimely death in Ongar Ridge. As he had grown towards manhood, Paul Peters had felt an overwhelming curiosity to know what had happened after the two brothers had joined the Confederate cause.

Men returning after the hostilities were generally not inclined to discuss the horrors they had endured and witnessed, and his mother's neighbours had only been able to provide a limited amount of information about what had happened to the group of ten Virginians who had set off together when two-year-old Paul and his mother had waved farewell to his father and uncle all those years ago. They knew that the group of neighbours had joined Jeb Stuart's Confederate cavalry troops and were involved in various conflicts prior to arriving to engage in the Gettysburg hostilities.

Other than confirming his father's death, the intriguing letter his mother had produced had not given any details of their involvement in that battle and had simply added to Paul's need to learn something more about the crime which had caused his uncle to flee west.

Now that he was sure he had re-established a link to his uncle, he was determined to find out whatever he could, even though he had arrived too late to question him in person. Why had his uncle never returned home after the war? What had led him to far-away Ongar Ridge instead?

Paul Peters simply hoped that staying in the Texas town and using a newspaper as a kind of investigative base might help him answer some of the questions swirling around in his mind. Above all else, he wanted to discover what had happened on the early morning of his uncle's death in the print shop, and hopefully find out who was responsible.

5

It took Paul Peters and young Jake Thornton a full three days to clear up the mess in the print shop. Although he was unsure of his alphabet, the youngster quickly came to differentiate between the different upper and lower case letters and to copy the order in which each piece of metal type should be arranged in the wooden racks. He quickly came to recognize, and be able to name, the different type faces.

Together the two of them were just finishing the tedious clear-up task when Red Roberts appeared in the print shop doorway.

'What you doin' in here?' he demanded. 'Returnin' to the scene of your crime? Isn't it enough that you killed Jackson without interfering in here? Who said you could?'

'Not that it's any of your business,

Roberts, but actually I've got permission from lawyer Fisher. The print shop is his and I'm thinking of continuing to run it for him.'

'What? Spreading more lies? Especially about me and my brothers? Jackson was always keen to use his rag to tell everyone when that stupid Marshal Rowland had locked us up for the night just for havin' a bit of fun after a few drinks. Real killjoys both of them — the marshal and the newsman. Often been tempted to put a bullet in 'em. Perhaps I ought to put one in you before you go makin' trouble. No one will blame me, since most of the folk think you're a murderer anyways. That judge didn't do his job properly, letting you off like that without a real trial.'

As he spoke, Roberts moved his right hand towards his holster but used his left to grab the rack which had just been filled with the carefully ordered metal type. With a snort he tilted it so that, once again, the slugs of metal were spilled over the floor.

Angered, Paul Peters moved forward. 'Was it you who did that before?' he asked. 'When *you* killed Mr Jackson?'

'Keep your distance if you don't want a bullet in you,' said Roberts as he started to draw his Colt, but he was too late. Peters lunged forward, and with a rubber mallet used by printers he knocked the weapon to the ground and grabbed Roberts by the throat.

Roberts threw a wild punch which connected with his opponent's jaw and pushed him back against the wooden workbench. The two men exchanged blows in a vicious tussle until Roberts slipped on a piece of loose metal type and fell to the ground, striking his head against the bench as he did so.

He lay prostrate, with blood trickling from a deep gash in his forehead.

'Quick, go get the doctor,' Paul Peters asked Jake Thornton, as he realized Roberts was not moving. 'And get the marshal as well.'

Both arrived at the same time, and Doc Sullivan set about examining the unconscious man.

Marshal Rowland asked what had happened and got the same story of events from Paul Peters and his young assistant.

'And this Colt I've picked off the ground belonged to Roberts?'

'Yes, Marshal. I wasn't armed while I was sorting the type. He was drawing it when I made a move towards him.' Peters turned to the sawbones. 'How is he, doc? Will he live?'

'Reckon so — though that's perhaps more than we can say for you when his two brothers hear about this. They'll be after you for sure, and I wouldn't like to be in your boots when they catch up with you.'

★ ★ ★

Careful to remain armed after the doctor's sensible warning, Paul Peters spent a considerable amount of time reading through old copies of the *Ongar Tribune*, which enabled him to see what editorial issues his uncle had covered, and to find out who might have been sufficiently angered to have wanted the editor silenced.

The biggest issue concerned the area's main landowner, Antonio Garcia.

His land was largely used for cattle grazing, but he had added a variety of crops, and for these he needed an increased supply of water. His land was fed by a river which lay to the north-east of Ongar Ridge, but a smaller offshoot to this river had branched down to the town itself and Garcia had caused concern by damming that section and leading the water on to his cultivated area. The result was that the townsfolk were angry and fearful that, over time, their supply of water would be insufficient.

Their complaints had been callously rebuffed by Garcia. His attitude, reported in the *Ongar Tribune*, was simply to say that the townsfolk should dig deeper wells or buy water from him. Peter Jackson had staged an on-going newspaper campaign to get the land-owner to change his mind and allow the river to revert to its original course.

Marshal Rowland told Paul Peters that the editor had been forcibly warned to mind his own business. Apparently, on one occasion, three Garcia men had ridden into town to deliver the message that his life would be worthless if he printed one more word against their boss.

The other major issue concerned the town's mayor, Eustace Trimble. His store held a near monopoly on trade in the town and he had originally been generous in allowing townsfolk and local homesteaders credit on their purchases. Having allowed them to build up debts, he had then put the squeeze on them by saying that they would have to pay substantial interest if they didn't clear their debts within laid down periods of time.

Editor Jackson had written in the *Tribune* that this effectively increased Trimble's profit on goods he had sold earlier. Angered, Trimble had retaliated by withdrawing advertisements from the news-sheet and also cancelling other jobbing print work.

Marshal Rowland confirmed that the two men had been seen arguing loudly in the main street and it was obvious that there was continuing bad blood between them.

With the Roberts brothers, as well as Garcia and Trimble, it was clear to Paul Peters that he already had no shortage of suspects when listing those who might have wanted Peter Jackson out of the way.

★   ★   ★

Much of the local history he had read in the newspapers was confirmed when Paul Peters paid a second visit to Bessie Pullman.

At first, she was more than eager to extol the virtues of her former lodger.

'He seemed to have an overwhelming zeal to put right what he considered to be wrong-doing,' she said. But she then frowned and declared that Jackson was what she described as 'a deeply troubled man'. Surprisingly frank in her discussion, she revealed that he often suffered disturbing nightmares. 'He used the word 'atonement' but I never knew what he meant by it,' she said.

Her attentive listener wondered if this was somehow a clue to the JUSTICE notice pinned to the dead man's body.

Paul Peters already knew that his uncle had suffered a severe crisis of conscience after the civil war. The letter he had written to his sister-in-law, Laura, had revealed some of the truth, but also raised more questions. Was it perhaps possible that someone held a grudge against the editor for something that had happened earlier, rather than for more recent events?

He had written that he had a guilty past and suggested that his life could be in danger if someone from the past caught up with him. Could there be someone in Ongar Ridge who knew the hidden truth and had taken revenge in the print shop on that dark dawn?

6

Early one morning, Paul Peters decided to inspect the Garcia ranch and see for himself what the issue of river damming was all about. He went first to the marshal's office to tell him his intentions but saw only the deputy marshal.

'Sure you want to go sticking your nose into that business?' asked Luke Granger. 'Garcia likes keeping his land private. You won't be welcome.'

'I'll take that chance. Please tell the marshal where I've gone.'

He rode for nearly two hours, covering a variety of ground and flora as he climbed gradually away from the mesquite-covered lower level to the north of the town. Rounding the range of low-lying hills which had given Ongar Ridge its name, he passed several notices bearing the same message: *Private property. KEEP OUT*.

When he reached the disputed river location it was obvious what the problem was. Where the water had originally run through a deep cutting in the ridge and then down to the town, it had been dammed with rocks and the course turned back on to Garcia's land.

This meant that there was no direct supply to Ongar Ridge itself, which had grown up on the river banks. There were further ramifications, however, as the river had then continued through land which had been used by home-steaders who had taken over plots for livestock and cultivation. These were now reliant on smaller creeks, which were gradually drying out in summer droughts. What had originally been ideal territory for immigrants looking to build a better life was, in many cases, now providing a less promising prospect.

Satisfied, Paul Peters started back towards the town, but as he rode round an escarpment there was a rifle crack and the ground close to him was kicked up. He was either receiving a very pointed warning or was actually under real attack. As he quickly rode into a sheltered area in the rocks, four more shots came in his direction and they seemed to indicate that there was more than one gunman. He knew he was trapped, since there was no way he could re-emerge into the open without again making himself vulnerable to attack from the hidden bushwhackers.

He reckoned that his only safe plan was to stay put until dark, and then try to make his escape, using the light from the moon resting in a cloudless Texas sky.

As he settled ready for a watchful couple of hours before dusk, he was surprised to hear several more shots coming from the direction of the earlier salvo. He had assumed that he had been shot at by men paid to keep strangers off Garcia's land, but this time the shots did not seem to be aimed in his direction, and they did not continue for more than a couple of seconds.

Puzzled, he decided to remain in his hidden position. He stayed watchful and, after a while, saw three horses appearing from the further rocks. The riders came on to open ground and were heading in his direction without seeking cover. As the figures drew closer he recognized that the leading horseman was Ongar Ridge's marshal, Mike Rowland, leading two others. As they got even closer, the marshal yelled out: 'It's OK, Peters. It was the Roberts brothers shooting at you. This one beside me is Ned, with my bullet in his leg.' Pointing at the body draped over the back of the third horse, he added: 'His brother Jed is dead. Shot whilst resisting arrest.'

* * *

As the marshal, the captive Ned, and Paul Peters rode back to town together, Mike Rowland explained the background to the shooting.

'After Luke Granger told me you had

ridden out this way, I spotted the two brothers heading out of town in a real hurry. I wanted to know what they were up to, so I followed them. As they headed for the Ridge, I guessed they were after you as revenge for what you did to Red when you fought in the newspaper office.'

Peters cut into the narrative. 'But how did they know where I was going? I told no-one except your deputy.'

'Exactly,' said the marshal. 'But you ought to know that Luke Granger and the Roberts brothers have been acting close for some time. I'm sure you are aware that Luke has been saying the same as them: that you must have been the one who killed Peter Jackson and that Judge Kane was wrong to let you go free. Guess Luke told the brothers where you were going. I had to intervene if they were to be stopped from killing you.'

'They certainly weren't intent on wishing me a happy stay in your town, Marshal. What actually happened back there? They really had me holed up. I was waiting for dark to try to escape.'

The marshal shrugged. 'You might have got away with it, but I wasn't sure I could risk it. I came up quietly behind the two of them and ordered them to drop their weapons. They didn't do so, though. Both turned towards me and I had to shoot in self-defence. Hoped to wing both of them. Bad luck for Jed that he moved as my bullet reached him. Got him right in the chest. Ned was luckier. He's just got a leg wound.'

'Thanks, Marshal. Sounds as if I probably owe you my life, though I'm surprised they were determined to kill me just for injuring their brother in the print shop fight. Seems a bit extreme, don't you think?'

'Not really. The three brothers have always stuck together. It doesn't really shock me that they would act that way. They've been a nuisance ever since they arrived in my territory, and paying you back for hurting Red would certainly have been in character, even though an

70

attempted killing is more serious than anything they've done before. But, on the other hand, they could have had a stronger reason for wanting you out of the way. The tip-off from my deputy would have given them the perfect opportunity to get rid of you if they thought you were some kind of threat, and killing you out there was a pretty savvy thing to do. Could have been quite a while before anyone even knew you were missing, let alone dead.'

Thoughtful, Paul Peters acknowledged that the ambush had certainly demonstrated that the Roberts brothers had something to fear from the questions he had been asking in his attempts to get at the truth behind the editor's death, and now Jed's death would undoubtedly multiply the two remaining siblings' hatred of the self-appointed investigator. It was clear that he would have to step carefully.

But, in addition to fearing the two brothers, Peters considered it likely that the deputy marshal, Luke Granger, was not someone to be trusted. Could it be that he had some reason for not wanting closer investigation into the editor's death? Should the deputy's name be included in a list of murder suspects?

He questioned Mike Rowland and was told that Granger had been in the town for some while. Unmarried, he had originally arrived with a small group of immigrants but had quickly decided that he was not cut out for the tough life of a farmer. He had got a job working for Eustace Trimble, but had then been appointed as deputy marshal three years ago.

'I've got no complaints,' attested his boss. 'He's done a good job. No reason I know of that means you can't trust him.'

Despite this reassurance, Paul Peters decided to keep his suspicions alive.

7

The burial of Jed Roberts was a low-key event, which was not entirely surprising since few in the town or the surrounding district had felt much respect for any of the three brothers. The trio had arrived six years earlier, claiming they were prospectors who had hit it lucky with a strike 'over in Cochise County, in Arizona Territory'. Although they were never specific about the details, their boast may have had a truthful basis, since they seemed to have enough capital behind them to allow them the luxury of not having to work. They had taken over a derelict shack just outside town and had done little to improve it except for patching up the leaking roof.

Their trips into town to collect supplies usually involved them leaving their purchases in the care of the livery owner so that they could get themselves into a saloon, play cards, spend time with a couple of ageing whores and then get thoroughly drunk — often finishing up in the marshal's cell.

Amongst the few mourners at the burial graveside was Eustace Trimble, standing next to Marshal Rowland. Across from them were Ned and Red, both showing signs of their injuries, with Ned using a crutch and Red sporting a large bandage around his head. No legal action had been taken in respect of either the fight in the print shop or the bushwhacking incident. The marshal's killing of Jed was condoned when he claimed it happened whilst he was trying to undertake a legal arrest, and Ned was not in a position to contest that because he was not going to incriminate himself by admitting that the marshal's shooting was as a result of the two brothers' attack on Paul Peters.

It was perhaps invidious that Peters himself attended the burial, deliberately

74

standing opposite the brothers and attracting their hostile stares throughout the brief interment service. When it concluded, he quickly moved over to the marshal and mayor, so as to protect himself against the risk of the two brothers taking action to underline their fury at his unwelcome presence. After further hostile staring, they stomped away, no doubt even more determined to take some kind of revenge for his contemptuous act of being present.

'Surprised to see you here, Peters,' commented Mayor Trimble. 'Don't consider you to be one who would mourn the death of a man the marshal says tried to kill you.'

'True enough, Mr Trimble, but I could perhaps equally express some surprise, sir, that you would give up your valuable time to be here.'

The mayor did not reply immediately, but then justified his presence by muttering a few words about feeling it his civic duty to respect the departure of any of the district's citizens.

'Even troublemakers or crooks, Mr Mayor?'

At this extra challenge, Trimble visibly angered. 'Who says the Roberts brothers are crooks?' he demanded. 'Better be careful before you go making wild accusations. Suppose you'll be calling me a crook, too, like Jackson insinuated in that damn newspaper of his . . .'

'I would be happy to talk to you about that,' interrupted Peters.

He got no answer, however, except for a look of real ire from the mayor before he turned and hurried away without a backward glance.

Marshal Rowland laughed. 'Almost looked as if you hit a nerve there, young man, but you had better watch your step if you are planning on making an enemy of our senior citizen. Remember money talks, and he's got plenty to buy himself ways of exercising power.'

'Point taken, Marshal, but sometimes words in print can be even more powerful than money.'

'Maybe, but money can also buy bullets, and newsprint is no protection against them. So, like I said, you watch your step or you could end up getting hurt or even killed. Ongar Ridge is a pretty civilized place these days, but there are still a few people around who aren't averse to violence as a way of settling arguments. Unlike many other places, we've not made a ruling that guns have to be deposited with me when people are in town, so there's always the danger that personal disputes can end up with a shooting. Usually, though, fist fights are as far as it goes.'

* * *

As it happened, the marshal's words of warning turned out to be prophetic as early as that same evening. Paul Peters was having trouble locking the rather rusty padlock to the print shop building when he became aware of a noise behind him in the semi-dark. As he turned, he was first punched in the back by one assailant and then viciously in the solar plexus by a second man. Badly out of breath, he hunched up and that left his chin in an exposed position ready to receive a huge upper-cut: and this was the prelude to a severe beating. He hardly managed to get more than a couple of token blows against his two opponents before collapsing to the ground, where he was viciously kicked. Falling into semi-consciousness, he heard one of his attackers say, 'That's enough.' The beating was over.

Dusk had turned to full darkness by the time Paul Peters had struggled back into an awareness of his position, down in the dust with pain racking every part of his body. It was the best part of another hour before he could start to drag himself over the ground in the direction of Bessie Pullman's house, so it was nearly midnight before, still on his knees, he was able to pummel on her door. He thought she was not going to answer, so he reached down to draw his gun with the intention of using it to knock louder. His holster, though, was empty. Clearly his attackers had taken his Colt.

He continued banging on the door, and eventually he heard widow Pullman demanding to know who was disturbing her night's sleep. He just about managed to shout loud enough for her to agree to open up. 'Good God. What on earth have you been up to?' was her shocked greeting.

The widow nursed Paul Peters for three days before he asked her to tell the marshal where he was. He had refused her offers to call in the doctor, insisting that he wanted no one else to know what had happened until he was ready to get back on his feet.

'You sure look as if you had a disagreement with someone,' sympathized Marshal Rowland when he arrived and saw the bruises on the face of Paul Peters. 'Hope the other fella looks the same way. Anything broken?'

'No. Pretty sure it's nothing too

serious, though they made a good job of putting me out of action for a while. Don't exactly feel like getting into the saddle for a few days.'

'Know who did it? You said 'they', so there was obviously more than just one of them. How many?' queried the marshal.

'Seemed to be just two. Caught me by surprise, so I didn't really get a good look at them before I was down. Pretty sure it wasn't either of the Roberts brothers, though. These two were bigger built. Any ideas, Marshal?'

'No one immediately comes to mind, though it was obviously someone anxious to stop you nosing around too much. Or someone who had been paid to give you a warning, of course.'

A rueful half-smile was evident on Paul Peters as he rubbed his aching side. 'If it was meant to be a warning, I wish they had just sent me a letter.'

'Would certainly have been less painful,' agreed the marshal, 'and at least that might have indicated who was behind the beating. You certainly haven't taken long to upset someone.'

'I can't justify saying this, marshal, but I've just got a hunch that it could be Trimble. He really acted rather strangely at the funeral, and he would certainly be in a position to dish out the dollars to get someone to do his dirty work for him. I've been reading a couple of articles my uncle wrote in the *Tribune* and he seemed to be hinting that the mayor was not a man worthy of his position. Don't suppose he would have been that forthright in his criticism unless he had some kind of evidence.'

'Now hold on there, young Paul. You can't go accusing Trimble yourself just on a hunch that there's more to him than being a hard businessman. If your uncle had some kind of evidence, then surely he would have printed it. He wasn't the sort of man who would hold back if he had uncovered something illegal, and you certainly can't go thinking that our editor was killed because of something he knew but couldn't print. And surely he would have come to tell me about it if he was aware of anything illegal. He was always one to argue that the law should be respected and that the guilty should be punished.'

'I know that, marshal, but your warning won't stop me trying to get at the truth and I'm certainly not going to let a beating frighten me off.'

★ ★ ★

Bessie Pullman had put the injured Paul Peters in the room his uncle had rented. Now she suggested that he retain it on a permanent basis, pointing out that a bit of payment would help her out financially. Her guest was more than happy to agree. He had come to like the woman who had unselfishly nursed him after the beating and he discovered that she was an excellent cook — a huge bonus for a man who loved his food. His only reservation was that he was unsure whether his landlady already had ideas about making their relationship more personal. Whilst he was bedridden they had talked at length about her life and especially about the time the editor was under her roof.

Emboldened by the intimate nature of their discussions and aided by a shared bottle of whiskey, Paul Peters had dared ask if the couple had been lovers. Without any obvious embarrassment, Mrs Pullman answered that she wouldn't consider that the term 'lovers' was really appropriate. She added, however, that they had occasionally shared a bed. 'Men are not the only ones who have physical needs,' she added. As she spoke, she gave her listener an intense look which seemed to suggest that he might like to consider a similar relationship.

Peters chose to move the conversation on to what he considered to be safer ground by asking her an unrelated favour. 'Would it be possible for you to invite Eustace Trimble to come over for a meal, without letting him know that I am here?'

Bessie Pullman laughed out aloud. 'I don't think that would be a problem,' she said, 'though I think he'll most likely jump to a wrong conclusion. As a single man, he has often hinted at the possibility of the two of us getting together. More than hinted, in fact. But I've always resisted his advances. I think he's a self-centred, obnoxious character, if you want to know. So he's bound to convince himself that I've changed my mind about him. I'll deliver a written invitation for tomorrow night.'

★   ★   ★

Within an hour of the invitation being handed to the mayor's housekeeper, young Jake Thornton acted as a paid delivery boy, bringing a message that Eustace Trimble would be delighted to accept, and very much looked forward to what he hoped would be 'a very congenial occasion'.

When she showed the reply to her new lodger, Mrs Pullman chuckled like a schoolgirl. 'I wonder what he considers to be the meaning of that word,' she mused. 'He certainly won't think it means a meeting with you. Should be an interesting evening.'

★ ★ ★

When the town mayor came knocking on Mrs Pullman's door dead on the appointed time, he was dressed in his very best city suit. He carried a bottle of champagne in his hand, but nearly dropped it when he stepped inside and saw Paul Peters lounging in the widow's most comfortable chair.

'What the hell are you doing here?' he sputtered. 'Thought you'd left town after that beating . . . '

'Good evening, Mr Trimble. Didn't Mrs Pullman tell you I was also to dine with you? Personally, I've been very much looking forward to it. I'm told you're a very interesting man and are very knowledgeable about all sorts of things. How, for instance, did you know that I had been attacked?'

Trimble reddened, clearly surprised at Peters' presence and by his sudden blunt question. The man demonstrated that he was a quick thinker, however, by conjuring up an answer after only a short pause. 'Just a matter of putting two and two together,' he said. 'I was told that Mrs Pullman had been buying bandages in my store. When I wondered who they were for, my clerk mentioned that he had been told you hadn't returned to the hotel, and now I see bruises on your face it is fairly easy to guess that someone put them there.'

Impressed by Trimble's hasty recovery, Peters tried to regain the initiative. 'As the most influential man in Ongar Ridge, perhaps you could hazard a guess as to who might have felt the need to rough me up?'

'Why ask me? Don't you know? I'm surprised you can't identify him if you had a little fight, and I'm certainly surprised that you expect me to be able to suggest a culprit. I don't make a habit of mixing with ruffians.'

Paul Peters found himself even more impressed. Either Trimble genuinely didn't know that there had been two assailants, or he was clever enough to deliberately conceal detailed knowledge about the attack. If he was in any way responsible, then he had skilfully clouded the issue by talking about only one attacker.

What was surprising was the way the mayor continued to act throughout the evening in a confident, and even jovial, manner. After his initial shock at encountering Paul Peters, he acted as if he was quite unperturbed at finding himself in a party of three rather than enjoying an eagerly anticipated cosy supper for two. He chatted freely about town matters and also about his own background, and with some obvious pride outlined his own successes as a businessman. He explained how he had arranged contracts with various suppliers, including contacts with traders in his home town of Chicago. 'After that city's disastrous fire in October '71, Chicago has been rebuilding itself at an amazing rate,' he explained. 'The old wooden buildings that were burnt down have been mostly replaced by steel and concrete, and the owners of the destroyed businesses used the occasion as an expansionist opportunity. They built up a wide network of suppliers and customers as they went about reconstructing the city. Believe me, it is rapidly becoming one of the nation's greatest commercial hubs, dealing in everything from corn to metals, and I've got my own share of that growth. What I'm doing here in Ongar Ridge is small scale, but I've also established some profitable investment links.'

Although Trimble was seemingly happy to be boastful about his successes, Paul Peters noticed that he was more reticent when asked about his transport arrangements. His comments became deliberately vague when asked how he arranged the movement of goods across the country, and his listener determined that he would look into that when he got the opportunity. Despite Trimble's confident bluster, Paul Peters felt sure that the man was not truly as open as he appeared. Once again, he suspected that his uncle had somehow uncovered something improper that he had only been able to hint at in the *Ongar Tribune*.

All in all, though, the evening had produced nothing in the way of solid evidence. Certainly, Paul Peters had discovered nothing which in any way established links, or even clues, that would help him find a reason for his uncle's death. If Trimble was involved, then he had given no information that would aid the investigation.

8

The morning after the meal at Bessie Pullman's house, Paul Peters decided that it was time to announce that he was ready to start his own publication, operating under the banner title of *The New Tribune*. His decision was endorsed by lawyer Charles Fisher, and the next call was to the marshal's office where he found both Mike Rowland and his deputy, Luke Granger.

The marshal helped by passing on details of a couple of minor incidents which could be reported, but a morose Granger just stood scowling, obviously not excited by the news. Paul Peters decided to tackle the man directly. 'Why did you tell the Roberts brothers that I was riding out to the Garcia place?' he challenged.

He expected a denial, but Granger was able to avoid being caught out in a lie. 'Why shouldn't I have told them? They were in here soon after you told me what you was up to. They asked me what you wanted. I saw no harm in it, so I told them. I wasn't to know they would follow you, so don't go blaming me for what happened. Mike here said I should have guessed what might happen, but I didn't. So get off my back, mister.'

Granger turned and went out, slamming the heavy wooden door behind him.

'You two don't exactly happen to have hit it off,' commented Mike Rowland. 'But you know I'm still as determined as you to find out about your uncle's death.'

'Thanks, Marshal. You got any more ideas?'

'No. Sorry. Don't see how we are going to get any closer to it, either. Where are any clues going to come from?'

'Well maybe, just maybe, this might help. Might just jolt someone into

91

coming forward.' Paul Peters produced a proof copy of the front of his first news-sheet, and handed it to the marshal.

WHO KILLED
PETER JACKSON?

This is the first issue of a newspaper aimed at the citizens of Ongar Ridge and the surrounding district. It is intended to inform and to stimulate discussion.

Most of you will be aware that, as a newcomer to your town, I was wrongly accused of killing your esteemed editor of this publication's predecessor. I do not claim to have the experience or skill to emulate his high standards of journalism but I do hope to pursue the same aim of exposing any wrong-doing which impacts on your daily lives.

One of the prime current examples of such matters is the death of Peter Jackson himself. Anyone who has information that might reveal the truth is asked to bring it to my attention.

PAUL PETERS

'Don't know whether it will do any good, Marshal, but it might just tempt someone who knows something that they haven't told you about.'

'Maybe — but I doubt it. Certainly won't tempt a killer to come forward! Meanwhile, I'm going to visit the Garcia place tomorrow. Fancy riding out with me? You can show him your editorial.'

'That's great, Marshal. It will give me a chance to ask him about this water business. But let's make sure no Roberts brothers are on my tail this time. I don't fancy being bushwhacked again. Not even with you alongside me!'

★ ★ ★

They set out early, and by mid-morning had already arrived at the fencing that bounded the southern end of the considerable area of the Garcia ranch. As they opened the gate below the arched entrance, they could see two riders approaching them. 'They'll be our escort,' commented Mike Rowland. 'It's standard practice and a sign of how many men Garcia has at his disposal. I was surprised no one got on to you last time when you rode in alone.'

The two Mexican riders knew the marshal by sight and little was said in reply when he told them he wanted to see their boss, but they acted as a close escort for the further ride up to the ranch house.

Paul Peters was mightily impressed by the Spanish-style hacienda. It obviously had some history behind it, compared with all other buildings in the district, and indicated the local significance of its owner.

Surprisingly the man himself was on the veranda entrance to welcome them, though it was not clear how he had been made aware of their approach. A large man, probably in his forties, Garcia was well dressed in an expensive version of a rancher's clothing, and held a huge cigar in his hand. Marshal Rowland formally introduced Peters, who was emboldened to ask how their arrival had been expected. With a smile, Garcia took his visitors through the grandiose entrance hall, up a wide staircase and on to an upstairs balcony where a young boy was sat behind a massive naval telescope.

'Mr Peters, one of my pastimes is astronomy. At night I observe the heavens, and during the day the sons and daughters of my retinue act as an efficient warning system to make sure we get no unwelcome visitors. They are well paid for their duties, as well as getting professional school tutoring. I look after my people.' There was obvious pride, rather than boastfulness, in their host's explanation.

'Why do you feel you need such precautions?' asked Peters.

'I wish I didn't, but you ought to

know that the original ranch set up by my father has been gradually reduced by newcomers eating away at my land. In addition to the homesteaders, I've had constant struggles with rustlers and have been forced to fence off part of what was legitimate free range. My herd has been reduced because of the restricted grazing, and I have had to diversify into crop growing rather than rely on beef.'

'And that's why you altered the water course?'

Suddenly Garcia's tone sharpened. 'Too damn true I have. I need all the water I can get and I have to stop others thinking they can come in and take more of the land my father fought so hard to establish. Like him, I'll also fight to defend what's mine, if I have to. So don't you go encouraging more trouble from those who think I'll just roll over and let them take whatever they want. I aim to keep what's mine, and no town council, no newspaper, no marshal, or no court is going to alter that.' In case his outburst sounded too incriminating, Garcia modified his stance a little by adding that he had resisted the illegal actions taken by other cattle men who had found their land grabbed. 'Let me tell you I've not gone in for the barn burning, or worse, that other landowners have done, but I sure don't intend to keep turning a blind eye to the continuing pressures on my legitimate rights.'

Garcia emphasized his point by banging on the oak table where an expensive whiskey decanter had been placed together with three glasses. 'Now normal hospitality rules suggest I should offer you two gentlemen a drink, so let me pour you one, but while I do so, perhaps you would tell me why you rode out here uninvited.' The stress on the final word made it pretty obvious that the earlier courteous welcome should not be taken at face value. The menace was obvious, and Marshal Rowland wisely lowered the temperature with a conciliatory warning.

'Just came to warn you that I've had information that a group of bandits have hijacked a supply wagon heading from Austin. They killed the two men on it, so you might want to be extra alert for a while.'

'I'll do that, Marshal. And what about you, young fella? What's that bit of paper you've been holding in your sticky paw? Something you want to show me?'

Wordlessly, Paul Peters handed over the yet-unpublished editorial. Garcia read it carefully, and then dropped it on the table, rather than handing it back. He gave a deliberate long sigh before commenting. 'I make no secret that I wasn't too happy at some of what Jackson wrote, sticking his nose into matters that were no concern of his. And I won't pretend I'm particularly saddened by his death, but you have my word that his killing is something I know nothing about. So you can look elsewhere if you insist on making it your business.'

* ★ *

On the ride back to Ongar Ridge, again accompanied by two of Garcia's hands as far as the ranch boundary, Paul Peters pondered over the somewhat mixed reception they had received. 'Strange man,' he summed up his feelings to the marshal, 'but somehow I believed him when he said he had nothing to do with my uncle's death.'

Mike Rowland did not reply. His attention was focused instead on a buggy coming towards them from the direction of the town. 'I recognize that,' he said. 'It's Trimble. Let's hold up and have a word with him.' But it did not work out that way, for when the buggy reached them Trimble simply waved and rode straight on past them, clearly having no intention of stopping to converse.

'Strange,' said the marshal. 'He must be heading to the Garcia place. Wonder what the connection is. Didn't think those two had anything in common.'

* * *

When *The New Tribune* was published and distributed, it was received with no great acclaim. After the Sunday church service a couple of people spoke to Peters, but no one mentioned his appeal for information relating to the mystery of Peter Jackson's death. It was almost as if most people regarded it as a rather insignificant part of history, certainly of less immediate concern than news of the bandit raid on a supply wagon.

Paul Peters had got this story from Mike Rowland, who had pointed out that it was not the first time supply wagons had been attacked. It was clear, however, that this information was more important to Ongar Ridge's citizens than the editorial appeal relating to Peter Jackson.

This lack of response added to the new editor's growing feeling of despondency.

* ★ ★

After reading the letter his uncle had
sent to his mother, Paul Peters had set
himself the improbable task of travelling to the broad expanse of Texas in
the hope of tracing a man he hadn't
seen for nearly twenty years and whom
he knew was living under a false
identity.

By some quirk of luck, or even
pre-ordained fate, he had found the
location of his quarry, but had arrived
just a few hours before the man's
premature death. Peters cursed himself
for the extra day he had spent in San
Antonio making his enquiries about a
man with a Virginian accent who was
believed to be playing some kind of
public role which his letter home
seemed to indicate was intended as an
attempt at redemption.

As in previous townships he had
ridden through, Peters had asked the
editor of the San Antonio newspaper if
he had any knowledge of a man who

might have arrived sometime after the civil war, and was now perhaps operating as a lawman, a town official, or even in a religious capacity. The editor, who perhaps sensed a story he could use in his own newspaper, had thrown out a few suggestions. These had included a man named Peter Jackson who had taken up running a campaigning newspaper in the smaller town of Ongar Ridge. Immediately Paul Peters had recognized the possibility that 'Peter Jackson' was a pseudonym for Jack Peters. He remembered that, as a very small child, he had sat with his uncle and had been intrigued by the string of letters which could be formed into words, which in turn could produce sounds and meanings. His uncle clearly had a love of playing with words, and it would have been entirely within his character to have twisted his real name into an alternative he could use in his new life.

Armed with this thought, it was with considerable excitement that Paul

Peters had set out from San Antonio to cover the short distance to Ongar Ridge.

On arrival, however, he had not immediately sought out the man who might be his uncle, deciding to leave it until the following morning after getting some much needed rest. How he now bitterly regretted that delaying decision, which meant he would never meet the fugitive he sought, and that the few extra hours he had delayed would even result in his own arrest for the murder of the man he had felt sure was his long-lost relative — a fact which had been confirmed by the marshal's acceptance of the story of the editor's injured hand.

*　*　*

In his short time in Ongar Ridge he had suspected various people as being responsible for his uncle's death. Had it been ordered by Mayor Trimble because of some kind of devious deal the editor had uncovered? Was the rancher Garcia somehow involved? Could one of the Roberts brothers have been responsible? And what about the deputy marshal? There were too many suspects, but not a shred of evidence to directly link any of them to the death in the newspaper office. Would he ever get to the truth?

9

One evening, Bessie Pullman's bakery assistant, Jessica, came to the widow's door in a desperate state. Her face was bloodied and she was doubled up in pain from her stomach.

'What on earth has happened?' asked Bessie, as she helped the young woman into a comfortable position and prepared to patch up her surface injuries. Jessica burst into tears. 'It was William. He went berserk — just because his meal wasn't ready when he wanted it. I had to escape or I think he might have killed me. I ran out when he was getting the whiskey bottle.'

As she spoke, her husband burst in through the door. 'Thought I might find you here, you lazy bitch,' he fumed and moved into the room towards Jessica. He grabbed her arm, and slapped her across the face with a vicious blow that sent her reeling in one direction, whilst also pulling her arm in towards him so that her shoulder was wrenched in its socket.

Paul Peters jumped to his feet. 'Hold on there, fella. You can't do that.'

William Shackleton threw the girl to one side and turned to face Peters. 'Don't you tell me what I can and can't do with my own damn woman. None of your damn business. Thought I taught you a lesson before. Don't you learn? Want another beating, do you?'

The blacksmith swung a mighty blow towards Peters, who was able to dodge it with ease, and land his own punch into his assailant's midriff. He followed up with a solid right-hander to the man's jaw. Despite the blacksmith's considerable size advantage, two more quick follow-up blows sent him staggering backwards, causing him to crash the back of his head against a shelf fixed to the wall. Stunned, but still standing, the giant lumbered towards Paul Peters with flaying arms which did no more than glance off the lighter man's body.

Much more nimble on his feet, Peters stepped to one side and then closed in to land a series of swift blows to the blacksmith's body.

Again the man staggered backwards, sending furniture flying. He tripped over an upturned chair. This, however, brought him into contact with Jessica, who had been crouching against a wall. He grabbed the terrified girl in a bear hug. 'Stand back,' he ordered Peters, 'or I'll squeeze the life out of this useless bag of horse dung.'

Paul Peters had no choice. He had to stop his attack whilst he tried to figure out how to deal with the situation. The dilemma was solved by Bessie Pullman. With a yell of 'Gotcha' she brought a heavy rolling pin down on the back of Shackleton's head.

In what was almost a graceful movement, the blacksmith slid down the wall behind him so that he finished in a sitting position on the floor, having released Jessica as he went down.

Clearly out to the world, he looked as if he was simply sat down for a rest with his chin dropped forward on to his chest.

Paul Peters couldn't guarantee that this would remain the situation for long, however. With the rolling pin at the ready he asked Bessie Pullman to fetch some cord and the two of them quickly bound Shackleton and tied his feet to the table.

In fact it took their prisoner around twenty minutes to come round, with much moaning and groaning mixed with some choice expletives.

'Granger and me should have fixed you for good last time,' he spluttered, in a clear admission that it was the blacksmith and the deputy marshal who had earlier attacked Peters outside the print shop.

'Why did you beat me up before?'

'We were paid to do it, of course, to teach you to mind your own business.'

'And who paid you?'

'I ain't saying.'

'Well, you aren't moving from here until you do. No one knows you're here and you're not getting any food or water until you start talking. I've no sympathy for you after the beating you gave me — so you'd better resign yourself to an uncomfortable stay unless you start doing some explaining. Let's start with why you and your buddy killed Peter Jackson.'

That accusation certainly worried Shackleton. 'No way, Mister, are you going to pin that on me. I had nothing to do with that man's death, though he once wrote an unnecessary story about me in his newspaper.'

'What was that?' asked Paul Peters, but got an answer blurted out by the man's wife, rather than his captive.

'He wrote that William was a disgrace to the community with his frequent drunkenness. He reported that a couple who wanted their horses shoeing had to wait all morning while William sobered up,' revealed Jessica.

Shaking the remaining dizziness from

his throbbing head, Shackleton snarled at his wife. 'You shut your mouth, woman. No need for you to repeat that nonsense.'

* * *

In fact it wasn't until past noon the next day that William Shackleton accepted that his captor had been serious in his threat. Cramped, thirsty, and with a splitting head caused by the blow from Bessie Pullman's rolling pin, he finally relented and started talking.

He admitted the assault on Paul Peters, and, under pressure, claimed that it was Mayor Trimble who had paid them in an attempt to stop the newcomer from continuing the *Tribune* criticisms previously printed under Peter Jackson's editorship. Shackleton categorically denied having anything to do with the editor's death, however, and he was adamant that he could provide witnesses to prove that he had been drinking and playing cards all night and right through into the morning until after Jackson's body had been found.

Somewhat reluctantly Paul Peters accepted that the man was probably telling the truth. It would be easy to check later whether Shackleton's alibis held up, and that he should therefore be erased from the list of murder suspects.

That still left questions around the beating Shackleton and Granger had administered. Ignoring the blacksmith's pleas to be released, his captor continued to question him. 'What was Trimble so concerned about, that he would pay you to try and silence me?'

'I ain't saying no more.' Despite his discomfort, for another two hours Shackleton did indeed refuse to add anything to his admission that it was Trimble who had paid them to carry out the beating. He clearly regretted his earlier angry outburst and wasn't eager to incriminate himself, Granger or Trimble any further. Finally, however, he became more desperate and decided to barter for his release.

'Let me go and I'll give you a hint. Just don't let on that it was me who told you!'

'Told me what? You haven't said anything useful yet, except that you claim it was Trimble behind my battering. What else you got to say, Shackleton? Give me a reason to let you go,' offered Peters.

'I ain't saying much. Don't really know too much, but Granger said something about us frightening you off in case you started nosing into the business of bandits holding up delivery wagons. Reckon there's a story there somewhere that it would be worth exploring. Now let me go, before I die of thirst.'

* * *

When he was released, Shackleton had trouble standing. It took him minutes to get the blood circulating in his cramped limbs, and he still held his head where the rolling pin had landed.

'You keep out of my way, and I'll keep out of yours,' he snarled at Peters. Then he turned to Jessica: 'You come with me, girl. We've got some talking to do.'

The young woman looked terrified. 'I'm not coming with you, William. Mrs Pullman says I can stay here with her and that's what I aim to do. You treat me like a slave and I've had enough of your drinking and bullying. You better get used to the idea that our marriage is over.'

Shackleton flared up and moved as if to grab his wife, but then changed his mind as he saw Bessie pick up the rolling pin.

He stumbled to the door, turned and shouted 'To hell with all of you,' before going out and slamming the door behind him.

After he had gone, Bessie Pullman continued to console Jessica, who had burst into tears. 'What have I done?' she asked.

'Nothing you need be ashamed of, my dear. It wouldn't be safe to stay under the same roof as that bully. Sooner or later he would have really hurt you. You are much better off here.'

Meanwhile Paul Peters pondered how he could best use the information that it was Shackleton and Deputy Granger who had been responsible for the beating he had been given outside the print shop.

10

On reflection, Paul Peters considered that he had enough evidence from Shackleton to confront Trimble. He went to the man's office above his emporium and burst in without knocking.

'What the hell do you want?' challenged the mayor, who was sat behind a hugely impressive desk with an array of area maps pinned to the wall behind him.

He stayed seated when Peters went up to the desk and stood over him aggressively.

'I've come to ask you some questions. And I want some straight answers.'

'Are you threatening me, Peters? You've absolutely no authority to barge in here like this, and I'll only talk to you if you remain civil. Why don't you sit down.' He gestured towards an expensive-looking ivory cigar box on the desk. 'And help yourself to a smoke if you fancy one.'

Eustace Trimble was back to the confident, unctuous behaviour he had displayed during the dinner at Bessie Pullman's house. Paul Peters decided on a straight attack in order to try wiping the smile off the man's face.

'Why did you order me to be beaten up by Shackleton and Granger?' he challenged, expecting a denial but trying to put the mayor under pressure.

Instead, Trimble merely continued smiling. 'Did it hurt? Did they do a good job? Did I get value for money?'

Peters could hardly believe the confident arrogance of the man. 'So you admit it was you ordered the attack?'

Trimble didn't answer immediately. He stood up and wandered round his office, taking his time to admire a large painting of an Indian encampment as if it was the first time he had bothered to study it. After a couple of minutes, he turned towards Peters. 'I thought maybe you needed a bit of a warning not to get too nosey. You came here, a complete stranger, get let off a murder charge, then start poking your nose into matters that are no business of yours. I thought a bit of roughing up might make you decide to move on. We don't need a nuisance newspaper in Ongar Ridge.'

Incensed by the man's arrogant coolness, Peters again decided on attack. 'Is that why Peter Jackson was killed? Did you arrange that the same way you arranged for me to be beaten up?'

This time Trimble appeared less at ease. He raised his voice and pointed a finger towards his questioner. 'Don't you go accusing me of that! I had nothing to do with that man's death. And don't you go printing anything that even suggests it.' His bombast abated and he seemed to relax again. 'And by the way, outside this room I will, of course, deny having anything to do with you getting a bit of a beating. In any case, who is going to take the word of a stranger who some folk still regard as a murderer, rather than the town mayor they voted for? What I've said in this room is between us.'

'But William Shackleton has admitted it was him, and that you ordered it, Trimble.'

The mayor sank back into his luxurious leather chair. 'Don't worry — he'll not be repeating that any more, especially in public. You've got no evidence against me, and I'm getting mighty tired of your cheek coming here like this, so get out before I call the marshal.'

Peters again tried to put the mayor under pressure. 'Or perhaps your friend, deputy marshal Luke Granger?'

This time Trimble looked just a little more concerned. 'Time for you to leave,' he said. 'And don't come accusing me of stuff again, or you might get more than a bit of a beating.'

Paul Peters was disappointed and dissatisfied with the outcome of the meeting, but was convinced that — despite his outward confidence — Mayor Trimble had something to hide.

He decided that he would also tackle Luke Granger, and made his way to the marshal's office. He found the deputy alone, sitting at the marshal's desk cleaning a Colt revolver, which Peters immediately recognized.

'That's mine. Why have you got it, Granger?'

The deputy looked up with a guilty expression, but his voice remained calm. 'Is it, now? You sure of that?'

'Yes, I'm sure. Why have you got it? Where did you get it?'

Granger hesitated, but only for a few seconds. 'Found it in the dust near the print shop, but I guess the marshal might let you have it back if you can prove it's yours. Bit careless of you to have dropped it, wasn't it?'

'Didn't drop it. It was taken from me — but you know something about that, don't you, Granger?'

As he spoke Marshal Rowland entered. 'I heard that and I think it's perhaps about time we let you into a couple of secrets. Tell him what you've been up to, Luke.'

Granger looked surprised. 'You sure, Mike? Why should we trust him? This is all complicated enough already, isn't it?'

The marshal perched on the side of the desk. 'Listen, Peters. The reason Luke has got your gun is that he took it from you when you got your beating. Didn't want you grabbing it and hurting someone.'

'Hurting someone?' blurted Peters. 'It was me that got hurt, and I know you were involved, Granger. William Shackleton has already admitted it was the two of you. Do you deny it?'

The deputy marshal looked to his boss, seeking approval. When he got a nod of acquiescence, he continued. 'No, I don't deny it. It's true that I was involved, but you're lucky I was. Shackleton was all for taking one of his blacksmith hammers and caving your head in.'

'So I'm supposed to be grateful, am I, that the two of you left me half dead!'

Mike Rowland took over the narrative. 'Better half dead than ready for the undertaker. Mayor Trimble wasn't fussy how far it went. Just said he wanted you to be taught a lesson.'

Paul Peters was baffled — and angry. 'So you knew that they were being paid to do it? And you, the marshal, let it happen. What kind of lawman are you? Are you being paid by Trimble, too?'

'Hold on, there, Peters, until you know the full story,' replied the marshal.

* * *

For the next half-hour the marshal and his deputy spoke at length about a plot to trap Trimble into revealing his guilty involvement in a complicated game which somehow centred on the rancher Garcia and the attacks on supply wagons.

They explained that Peter Jackson had come to them with information that there was a link between Trimble and Garcia and that the Roberts brothers were acting as go-betweens, paid for their services.

The editor had been in Trimble's store when Ned Roberts had come in, somewhat the worse for drink, and had shouted at Trimble that they were owed money for what he called 'the last job we done for Garcia'.

Peter Jackson was quite specific about what he had heard, but said he had found out nothing more because Trimble, realizing that there were customers listening, had told Roberts to shut up, and had then ushered him upstairs to the office.

Later that day, when the two men had passed in the main street, Peter Jackson had tackled Trimble about the bit of conversation he had overheard.

Trimble had told him, in no uncertain terms, to mind his own business, and threatened him that he would come to an unpleasant end if he ignored the warning.

'Do you think it was Trimble who murdered the editor?' the dead man's nephew asked the marshal.

'Very much doubt it, though it is certainly possible that he paid someone to do it, like he paid Shackleton and Luke here to give you a warning.'

'Marshal, I'm still sore about that. What the hell is going on when a lawman accepts money to beat up an innocent citizen?' Peters turned to the still-seated deputy. 'What the hell of a game is that? And I want my Colt back!'

'Sorry,' said the marshal. 'Sorry about the beating and sorry you can't have your gun back — not yet, at least. If Shackleton saw you with it, he'd know that Luke has been playing a double game. For some while Luke has been making out that he sides with the

Roberts brothers in thinking that you were the editor's killer. The idea was to trick them, or Trimble himself, into seeing Luke as some sort of ally. When Ned Roberts — acting for Trimble — offered Shackleton the job of looking after you, he suggested that Luke be approached to share in the beating. Shackleton was in debt from his gambling, and a deputy doesn't exactly earn a fortune. It looked like a good chance for both of them to make a bit of money, so Luke agreed to do it as part of our plot.'

'Good job for you I did,' interrupted Granger. 'Think there might have been a few broken bones, rather than bruises, if I hadn't got Shackleton to stop when he did.'

'Thanks a bundle,' said Peters with heavy sarcasm. 'So I'm supposed to be grateful for your protection when you actually punched and kicked the living daylights out of me!'

11

For two weeks, Paul Peters put production of his *New Tribune* in abeyance whilst he rode round the small-holdings mostly to the south of Ongar Ridge.

Although he had read several articles written in back issues of his uncle's newspaper, he was still amazed at the variety of nationalities and European languages he encountered as he visited nesters over a wide area. What they all had in common was a dream of a freedom from persecution and poverty, or perhaps prosecution, in their countries of origin.

Some could barely manage more than a few words in English, having come west from the eastern seaboard without having a chance to assimilate the language of their new country.

All, however, welcomed their visitor

with a degree of friendship and hospitality which often belied the hardened straits many were living under. With a mixture of English, their native tongue and — often — a degree of sign language, they were all eager to tell their stories, whether of success or struggle. Many had epic tales to tell of heading west in small groups, perhaps covering huge distances on foot with their meagre possessions or the livestock which had eaten up the limited capital they had disembarked with. Some of the earlier arrivals had tales to tell of dead companions — sometimes at the hand of Indian raiders.

Some had suffered losses at a later stage. Peters was particularly saddened by a pitiful set of headstones he was shown by one Swedish couple. The graves marked the deaths of all three of their children, aged three, six and eight years old, who had succumbed to illnesses they were unable to combat because of malnutrition.

Life was particularly harsh for the

women. The demanding tasks of clearing land, planting crops and caring for livestock was heavy work in support of their husbands. In addition they had the normal domestic duties of preparing and cooking food, keeping house, and bringing up children. For many, though, loneliness was their worst burden, as they had precious few opportunities to socialize.

All too often the dream of a better life was proving to be something of a delusion rather than a reality. Some told of families who had given up the struggle to wrestle a living from the land, and had headed back east to an unknown future.

Tactfully, Peters usually enquired about their rights to the land they had occupied and, in many cases, he was shown documents purporting to give legal possession. In truth, it was clear that the papers that were proudly produced were often worthless illegal claims sold to them by charlatans.

Other families or single men had no

papers but had simply settled on open range land which seemed to offer reasonable farming prospects. They trusted that homesteading a suitable piece of land gave them a legal right of possession. What was common to all was the importance of water, as well as fertile soil. Most had settled close to river tributaries, or at least land served by creeks fed from the north. Others had laboured to dig wells.

After two relatively dry years, all were now concerned by what was clearly a decreasing supply of the precious liquid which made their continued survival possible, let alone profitable. Some settlers, initially successful with their husbandry, were now operating at subsistence level as crops diminished and livestock lost their fat.

Despite the language problems, most of those Peters met had communicated with neighbours and had become aware that Garcia's damming of the main river to the north had at least contributed to their problems, and a hardening anger had built up.

The more literate had succeeded in getting their case reported by Peter Jackson and even in the Austin and San Antonio newspapers, but their attempts had achieved as little impact as a letter sent to the Governor. This had never been replied to, or even acknowledged.

Now, some of the more vociferous homesteaders were not shy to tell Paul Peters that their increasing desperation could easily lead to more direct action — without specifying, or perhaps even knowing, what form that action might take. The grudge against Garcia was palpable, even though most had no real idea who he was, or how they could combat the power he exercised over their futures.

What some of them could not understand was that Garcia had been allowed to act without himself facing any constraints or repercussions. 'Why hasn't the law acted against him?' one angry immigrant demanded. 'This is the sort of persecution we came across the seas to escape from. We came to build a better life for ourselves, but are not sure we can survive.'

Of more immediate concern, however, was their knowledge of the financial pressures most of them were under. They universally complained about the increased prices of the supplies they had to buy in Ongar Ridge, and were well aware that it was Mayor Trimble who controlled their future, almost as much as the weather. His pressures on them to repay credit loans, including interest, were mounting, and were often linked to threats that he would refuse to supply them with essential future goods.

Paul Peters returned to Ongar Ridge with a much heightened understanding of the economic realities of the area. He also had a fund of personal histories which could fill his pages for months if, indeed, he stayed around and kept the newspaper going. He knew that soon he had to make a decision about his own future.

He hankered to return east, but there was still the mystery of his uncle's dawn death to solve. Texas or Virginia?

* * *

One aspect of his return to the township after his tour of the surrounding country caused him a mixture of amusement and slight concern.

Both the widow, Bessie Pullman, and the blacksmith's estranged wife, Jessica, welcomed him as if he had been gone for years rather than a couple of weeks.

'I've really missed you,' shrilled Widow Pullman, as she helped him remove his boots. 'I must cook you a proper meal and . . . '

She was interrupted, however, by a hard stare and a heavily emphasized correction from Jessica Shackleton. 'We've both missed you,' she said.

As he washed away the traveller's grime he could hear the two women talking animatedly in the cooking area. It almost sounded like the first argument he had heard them have since the girl had left her husband. Whatever the debate was about, it resulted in a most welcome feast. With obvious pride, Bessie Pullman piled his dish full of beef, vegetables, steaming beans and, of course, bread from her bakery. When he had finished, he was about to light up one of his occasional smokes when Jessica came to the table with a huge apple pie which he was clearly supposed to tuck into. He was indeed being treated as some kind of returning hero.

* * *

Furthermore, the close attention continued into the night.

With his full stomach and saddle-weary limbs, Peters was near falling into a deep slumber when he was aware that someone had entered the room. Remembering the beating he had suffered earlier, his body stiffened as he realized that he had stupidly left his replacement Colt out of reach on a chair.

He was reassured, however, as a naked body slid in beside him and a female voice told him to 'just relax'. 'I don't want you wasting your money going to the whores in the Golden Bullet,' whispered Bessie Pullman, though her concern for his economic condition was clearly outweighed by a desire to satisfy his physical needs and, no doubt, her own as well. There was no objection from the Virginian.

12

A week later there was a less welcome nocturnal visit.

After his travels, Paul Peters had quickly published a copy of the newspaper in which he had reported the shortage of water that was so badly impacting on some of the farmers, and once again, he repeated the message that rancher Garcia was the direct cause of much of the hardship.

Clearly the criticism soon reached Garcia.

Jessica Shackleton rose from the table to open the door when a loud rapping indicated a visitor. In fact there were two visitors, and both burst in with guns drawn. One was a flashily dressed Texan and the other a swarthy Mexican.

With weapons pointed, both men looked as if they meant business and neither Bessie Pullman nor Paul Peters had any chance to react when the Mexican grabbed Jessica with his spare hand.

'I've come to deliver a simple message,' snarled the taller man, as he levelled his gun at Peters. 'You will not print any more stuff about Antonio Garcia and water supplies. Nothing more. You hear me?'

Paul Peters started to rise from his chair. 'But it's true that . . . '

'Sit down and shut your mouth. No more, I said. No more. Say nothing. Do nothing. It's not your business. Go back where you came from. And soon.'

Once again Paul Peters started to protest. 'I'm only printing the truth and . . . '

'Shut up. You will print nothing. And if you hang around you'll stop breathing also. You've been warned. And you might not be the only one who gets hurt.'

As he spoke, the Texan put his hand to Jessica's breast and ran it down her

135

body before opening the door so that both men could leave.

'You OK?' Peters asked a frightened-looking Jessica when they had gone.

'Don't worry,' she assured him. 'I've had worse. But I don't think you should fool around with those two, or with their boss.'

As the girl spoke, Bessie Pullman suddenly pointed excitedly at the window behind her. A red glow had appeared, and it was coming from the barn used for the production of *The New Tribune*.

Peters rushed to the door and was horrified to see that the whole building was burning. It must have been prepared for arson before the two unwelcome visitors had burst into the house, so it had needed only a couple of quick lights to set it ablaze before Garcia's men rode off.

The fire lit up the whole area, and although several men quickly came running from the main town towards the print shop, it was clear that nothing could be done to save the building or its contents.

With a sigh of resignation, Paul Peters acknowledged that the warning from Garcia's men had been accurate — at least as far as the end of printing operations was concerned. There would be no more *Tribune*.

He acknowledged that perhaps he ought to heed the Texan's second warning. It seemed to be a strong possibility that his life was in danger if he stayed in Ongar Ridge.

He wondered whether his uncle had ignored a similar threat and received a knife in his stomach as a result of his defiance.

Paul Peters found himself in a dilemma. He was no nearer being able to prove who had killed his relative, and he had no idea what he could achieve by staying in Texas. But he still held a nagging determination to try finishing the task he had set himself, as well as somehow continuing his uncle's work of exposing wrongdoings.

One of the first to arrive as the print shop burned was the town marshal, Mike Rowland. Along with others who had come with thoughts of helping, he soon accepted that any hopes of saving the building were pointless. The blaze continued fiercely, fuelled by the stacks of newsprint inside, and within minutes the roof collapsed on to the racks of type and machinery below.

After a while, Widow Pullman urged her devastated lodger to go back inside her house, and she invited the marshal to join them so that he could be told about the visit and the threats from Garcia's men. The marshal seemed hardly surprised, but expressed himself as unconvinced that much could be done about it. He listened to the descriptions of the two intruders and confirmed that they sounded like henchmen he had seen in town in the past.

138

'Well, why can't we ride out to Garcia's place and arrest them?' demanded Peters. 'Like I said before, you're the man wearing the badge. That's what your badge is all about, isn't it?'

'I understand your anger,' the marshal replied, 'but even if we got in there and came out alive, surely you don't think the two men you described would be sitting there waiting to be arrested. For sure, they would be nowhere to be seen. All we would achieve would be a denial from Garcia and a further warning to keep off his land. Anyway, I've got problems of my own to deal with.'

★   ★   ★

Marshal Rowland was certainly in a quandary. The previous night his deputy had been forced to enact one of his habitual arrests of Red Roberts. As usual the man had drunk too much before settling into a game of poker.

139

Without warning, he had fallen head first on to the table and scattered a sizeable pot and players' stakes on to the floor, with an argument then ensuing about how much money belonged to each player.

Recovering somewhat from his stupor, Red had started to claim that he was owed the bulk of the cash, and was threatening to throttle anyone who disputed his claim.

In a not unusual procedure, Luke Granger had intervened to frogmarch Roberts to the lock-up. This time, however, the process was a little different from the norm. As he was thrown into the cell, Roberts seemed to make a quick return to semi-sobriety. 'Luke, you can't lock me up. I've got a job to do. Gotta get to Garcia's place before noon.'

'Why?'

'Can't tell you, but it's important.'

'Well, if you can't tell me, Red, then you are staying exactly where you are until the marshal decides to let you go, and that won't be before tomorrow midday.'

Red Roberts suddenly looked really panicky. 'No, Luke, this is really important. You've got to let me go before then.'

'No way. You're staying.'

'Luke, you don't understand. They'll kill me if I don't deliver.'

Luke Granger realized his prisoner was really desperate, and that there was indeed something serious involved. He decided to trade on the idea that Red might accept that the deputy was not averse to earning an income supplement by involving himself in a bit of double-crossing. He recalled that it was Ned Roberts who had acted as Trimble's go-between when Luke had paired up with the blacksmith to give the stranger, Paul Peters, a beating.

'What's all this about, Red? What have you got to deliver? And what's in it for me if I let you go?'

Roberts considered his position. He asked the deputy for coffee to help him sober up, and then conceded that he had no practical choice other than trusting the deputy to keep quiet if he wanted his release.

'Can't tell you about it. It's a secret,' he said. 'But if you let me go I'll make it worth your while. I'm getting a coupla hundred dollars just to deliver a message. I'll hand it all over to you if you let me go. You can tell the marshal I sobered up and promised to pick up our supplies and leave town without causing more trouble.'

'What's the message, Red? You said you had to get to Garcia's place. Who's the message from, and what is it?'

'Can't tell you. Too risky, but have we got a deal?'

Luke Granger decided that he was not going to get more detail from Roberts and that the best strategy was to indicate that he was prepared to be bribed. He gave Roberts another strong coffee and accompanied him to the livery stable to make sure that he did indeed pick up his small supply wagon and head out of Ongar Ridge. He would be free to deliver his message to Garcia, though the deputy still did not know who the message was from or what important information it was to convey.

Keeping Roberts locked up was not going to shed any more light on the puzzle, but letting things develop might just lead to a clue, so the deputy decided that giving in to the pleading from his captive was the best course of action.

13

When Granger told Marshal Rowland about Red's urgent task, they were undecided what to do.

There seemed to be no point in riding out to the Roberts' shack or even following Red to Garcia's property. That wouldn't shed any light on the contents of the message, or what Garcia would do as a result of receiving it.

It was Paul Peters who came up with an outline plan. He had visited the marshal's office to tell Mike Rowland that he was thinking of leaving Ongar Ridge.

He had reluctantly accepted that he was no nearer achieving his objective of revealing his uncle's killer, and with the newspaper operation closed down, he now had no logical reason to stay. His intention, he told the marshal, was to visit the San Antonio editor he had met on his journey out, and encourage him to take up the story of the river damming and the effect it would have on the farmers to the south.

Peters was intrigued, however, when the marshal told him about the mystery of the message to Garcia.

'Seems to me,' suggested Peters, 'that the weak link is Roberts. He's erratic in his behaviour, is obviously money motivated, and knows more than he has let on so far. He obviously hates me from our earlier fight in the print shop. If I can engineer an encounter and get him steamed up, I might be able to get him to reveal something more.'

In fact, an opportunity occurred that same evening. Red Roberts had returned to town, presumably after completing his task of delivering the message to Garcia, and Peters spotted him coming out of the Golden Bullet and making his way to the marshal's office. Peters followed behind him into the office, where Roberts was fulfilling his promise to hand to Luke Granger the proceeds of his mission to Garcia.

Paul Peters closed and bolted the door behind him, stepped behind Roberts and stuck the barrel of his Colt into the man's back.

'OK, Roberts, now you're going to start talking. First, where did the money come from?'

'None of your damn business, Peters. Keep your nose out of this.' He then addressed Luke Granger. 'You tell him, Deputy, that we want him to keep out of our affairs.'

The deputy, however, quickly made his position clear. 'We've got nothing in common, Roberts. I only pretended to side with you in order to find out what you've been up to. Even beating up Peters here was part of a plan agreed with the marshal. Now you're going to talk.'

'And if I don't?'

'Well, first, I'll take your gun. Then I'm going to turn my back while Peters is given a chance to repay the beating you and your brother arranged. Then we're going to lock you up for a whole month without a sip of liquor.'

'You can't lock me up without a good reason.'

'Don't worry, Red, we'll have no trouble finding reasons. Now start talking. It was Trimble that paid you to take the message to Garcia, wasn't it?'

Roberts said nothing, but a simple nod of the head was all the confirmation that was required.

'And what was the message?'

'I ain't saying.'

'Was it written down?'

'No. I just had to remember it.'

'Remember what?'

'Told you I ain't saying.'

'That's a pity,' said the deputy, as he turned away. But it was a feint, because he quickly reversed his position and delivered a massive blow to Roberts' solar plexus. The man yelped in pain as he doubled up, only to get a chop on the back of the neck which made him stagger to one side and lean against the wall for support.

It took him a few minutes to recover enough to speak. 'You double-crossing bastard, Granger,' he spat out. 'I'm gonna kill you for this.'

'No, Roberts. You've got it all wrong. You're the one more likely to suffer. Now what was the message you had to deliver?'

As Granger raised his fist, preparing to throw another punch, Roberts decided that a little co-operation was perhaps preferable to more punishment.

'Won't mean anything to you,' he mumbled.

'Try me.'

'It was just a number.'

'What do you mean? What number? And what's it all about? Come on, spit it out.'

'It was just a number and a time. Mid-afternoon. That's why I had to get there before noon.'

'I still don't understand,' said Granger. 'What was going to happen mid-afternoon? And you still haven't told me what the number was.'

'It won't mean anything to you.' Red Roberts seemed to think it was almost amusing that he had a secret he wasn't going to reveal. He changed his mind, however, when he saw the expression of intent on the deputy's face as he raised his fist again.

'It was thirty-two,' he said.

'Thirty-two? What does that mean?'

'No idea. I just had to remember the number. Trimble made me keep repeating it, so I couldn't forget. Made me remember it in Spanish, too, so there was no mistake.'

'You know Spanish numbers?' asked a surprised Luke Granger.

'No, but he made me repeat the words. Sounded like tray-int-ta-ee-doss to me! But I told you it wouldn't help you. Now are you going to let me go?'

'No. You're staying until the marshal hears about this. Get in the cell.'

* * *

In fact the mystery of the number thirty-two was quickly solved when Marshal Rowland returned with the news that another two supply wagons had been attacked.

'When did it happen?' asked Paul Peters.

'Around mid-afternoon, apparently. This time there was an outrider above Comanche Pass where it happened. He saw the attack down below. He says a group of bandits attacked, killed the men on board, transferred the goods on to horses, burned out the wagons with the bodies inside, and headed off northwest. The outrider went back to Austin and told them what he'd seen. The sheriff is leading a posse to try to track the bandits. They'll probably hide out in the hills somewhere, though it's a mystery how they know when wagons are coming through. That's four attacks so far.'

As the marshal completed his briefing, the two law men were more than surprised to hear Paul Peters chuckle. 'I know,' he said enigmatically. 'And I know where they determine the best place to attack.'

He fell silent, savouring the look of amazement on his two listeners' faces. Finally he explained. 'They know when, and where, because they've been told by Trimble. That's what the message was all about. It was the time and the place.'

'But it was just a number,' commented Luke Granger.

'Yes. Just a number. But that number was one of many I noticed on the array of maps in Trimble's office. I'd bet good money that Garcia has a corresponding set of maps at his place. That's how he knows when a supply is coming through and the route it will take.'

Marshal Rowland looked thoughtful. 'It also explains a couple of things that have puzzled me for some while. It's quite an operation Garcia runs, with a lot of mouths to feed, yet his men hardly ever come into town for supplies. Even if they've got their own supply of meat and vegetables, they would still need other stuff. When I thought about it, I just assumed they went further afield rather than coming into Ongar Ridge, but I bet they get what they need from the wagons they attack. It's even possible that Trimble makes sure the wagons have whatever Garcia has ordered. It's all very neat.'

Luke Granger still seemed puzzled, however. 'But why would Trimble want supplies to disappear? It's costing him money.'

'I think I can explain,' said Peters. 'No doubt Trimble gets some payment from Garcia, but it also enables him to pretend to be the injured party and plead that he has to push up his store prices because of the losses he suffers when the raids take place. And that, in turn, is forcing some of the homesteaders to give up the struggle to survive so that they leave, and Garcia can grab back the land he considers is rightfully his. All round, it's a clever conspiracy between two wickedly selfish men.'

'OK, but that's enough talking. I reckon we ought to get going and see if we can join up with that posse,' decided the marshal. 'You coming, Peters? I reckon I can work out what route they'll take from Comanche Pass and why they've used horses and mules rather than just taking the wagons back with them. As a Ranger, I fought the Comanche in that area and know it well. They'll have taken a round route through passes in the rocky area where they would be difficult to track. Even now I think we'll be able to head them off and maybe lead the posse in the right direction.'

'What about Red?' queried Luke Granger. 'We can't just leave him locked up.'

Marshal Rowland pondered the problem for a moment. Luke had a point, he conceded. If they let Roberts loose, he would no doubt head straight to Garcia to sound a warning.

'OK, Luke. You stay here and look

after things in town. Keep Roberts locked up.'

Paul Peters said nothing, but privately noted that this arrangement meant that the deputy would not be personally involved in confronting the lawbreakers who had attacked the wagons. He still had his suspicions about Luke Granger.

14

Rowland and Peters were both excellent horsemen. They rode hard but sensibly and Paul Peters was impressed by the route his companion took. He hadn't exaggerated when he said he knew his way around, as the direction in which he headed seemed to be well away from the reported scene of the ambush, but he seemed certain that he could find the route the bandits would have taken with their captured provisions.

Using almost hidden passes they climbed steadily into low hills which eventually put them in a commanding position with a good view of the narrow trail in the area below them. 'I'm fairly certain they'll be heading this way, probably to store stuff in caves a few miles from here', said the marshal, in what proved to be a fully justified calculation.

They had waited less than half an hour when Marshal Rowland pointed to the first horse coming round an escarpment, heading directly below where they were stationed above. Soon afterwards this lone rider was followed by the rest of the raiders, each leading animals loaded with the bounty taken from the supply wagons.

'What now?' asked Peters.

'Well, unfortunately, there's no sign of the posse behind them. We can only guess that they didn't yet succeed in finding the tracks away from the ambush. But there's no way that lot can get past us without suffering heavy losses if we start shooting. Their only choice is to take shelter in the rocks down there or to turn back, and I'm guessing they won't want to head back in the direction they've come from and perhaps ride straight into the posse.'

'So it's down to us, then?' observed Peters.

'Shouldn't be too hard. How good are you with a rifle?'

'Good enough, Marshal.'

'OK. We'll let that lead rider pass, then we'll fire as rapidly as we can so that we can maybe fool them into thinking there's more than two of us. Hopefully we can keep going long enough for the posse to find their way to the noise. The rifle fire should echo pretty well.'

* * *

And that was the way it worked out.

When Rowland and Peters opened fire the lead horseman raced away unharmed, but two of the other riders were hit, along with three of the animals. Realizing that they were sitting targets, the other raiders dismounted and scrambled for shelter into the rocks.

For a while a few shots were fired up towards the two ambushers, but there was no way that they could be picked off from below.

'I reckon we can hold them down

there until a couple are brave enough to try and get up here — especially when it gets dark.'

In fact it was earlier than that when Mike Rowland spotted one of the men climbing up to their right. The bandit revealed himself long enough for Paul Peters to get off two quick shots and the man's body could be seen toppling back down — either dead or at least badly injured.

That seemed to be enough to deter others from attempting the climb, so that the confrontation simply turned into a stalemate. Occasionally one of the men sheltering below would fire upwards towards Mike Rowland and Paul Peters, who would then return a shot or two just to confirm that they were still in position.

The marshal again commented that it was likely the bandits would wait until dark before trying any kind of attack, particularly as they didn't know how many gunmen were keeping them pinned down.

In practice, however, the wait was not too long before the sheriff's posse of around twenty men arrived, no doubt attracted by the sound of gunfire. As they came round a bend in the ravine they immediately spotted the loaded animals which had stayed put despite the shooting.

As the posse dismounted and took up position, there was an exchange of bullets and two of the bandits were killed. That was enough for the other members of the gang to decide that, with the ambushers still above them and the posse outnumbering them, there was no point in resisting. A few further exploratory shots were fired, but it was obvious that the bandits were never going to be able to fight their way out. With hands raised they gradually appeared from amongst the rocks to surrender themselves to the sheriff.

Marshal Rowland yelled down his identity to his fellow law officer, and he and Paul Peters made their way back to their horses and then round and down to where the sheriff's team were getting ready to make their way back towards Austin with their captives and the recovered bounty.

The marshal recognized some of the captives as coming from Garcia's ranch. He explained how the lead bandit had taken off and the sheriff ordered one of his deputies to accompany the two men from Ongar Ridge on the ride to Garcia's ranch.

* * *

The three horsemen were soon picked up by two night riders when they reached the boundary of Garcia's land.

'We've come to see Garcia,' announced the marshal. The two guards exchanged a few words in Spanish, recognized Rowland and noted the deputy's badge on the posse member.

'OK You come with us.'

Once again, Garcia was waiting on the front porch when they got to the hacienda. This time he was dressed in expensive Mexican clothing. He ordered his two men to return to their duties and then challenged his visitors.

'I thought I told you that you were not welcome on my property. What are you doing here, especially at this time of day, or more accurately, time of night?'

Slowly, Marshal Rowland explained that they had just come from killing or capturing Garcia's men who had been involved in the raid on a supply wagon.

'How do you know they are my men?' challenged Garcia.

The marshal's voice was full of contempt when he said that he had personally recognized two of them, and that some of the others had already admitted to the sheriff that they worked for Garcia. In any case, the evidence for their raid on the wagons was indisputable. It was there on the loaded pack horses.

What he was not prepared for,

however, was Garcia's grounds for denial.

'If what you say is true,' he said, 'then I am truly sorry, but you will realize that I can't be responsible for what my men might have done without my knowledge. They choose to work for me but I can't — and don't — seek to control their lives. If they have really committed the crime you accuse them of then it is not my responsibility. If they have truly stolen other people's property they must have intended taking it to some sort of hide-out away from here.'

As Garcia mounted his verbal defence, the sheriff's deputy returned from the stable area. He had been looking for a sweated-up horse that would indicate that the lone lead rider of the bandits had returned to the ranch. He admitted, however, that there was no sign of the horse or its rider.

Garcia seized on this as evidence that the raid was absolutely nothing to do with him, and said he resented the accusation. Once again, he demanded that the three unwelcome visitors depart. 'That badge doesn't give you the right to keep coming here and making wild accusations, Marshal.'

Although frustrated by the lack of direct evidence against Garcia, Marshal Rowland felt confident that the Austin authorities would get some kind of proof from the captured men. He decided to say nothing about the map reference conclusion they had come to. Although this would hopefully be the proof to link Garcia to Trimble, he felt that it was an accusation best made later. Instead, he challenged the rancher about the Red Roberts visit. Surprisingly, Garcia made no effort to deny that he had seen Roberts.

'I pay him a little money to keep me informed of developments in town. Nothing significant but you are my neighbours, and even though I don't bother to come into town myself, I like to know what is going on.' With a sardonic smile, he added a comment to justify his stance. 'I understand, for instance, that the blacksmith's wife has left him and is living under the same roof as the newspaper man. I find domestic details like that fascinating.'

Feeling outmanoeuvred, Mike Rowland decided there was no point continuing the interrogation in this private setting, rather than later in a court of law. He was obviously not going to get any further with Garcia, so he turned to his two companions and suggested they all return to Ongar Ridge.

As they made to leave, however, there was the booming sound of a large explosion.

15

Garcia himself insisted on riding with them to investigate. As they approached the point where the main river had been dammed to re-direct the flow, it was soon apparent — even in the dark — that what had become a dried-up channel was now running with water.

'They've dynamited the dam,' exclaimed Garcia, as a round of shooting started.

At first it was difficult to determine the direction of the gunfire and impossible to know who was responsible, but then shouting from across the flowing water could be heard. The language was not easily discernible but the listeners could tell it was not English or even Spanish.

'Must be the European settlers, come to get the river flowing back down to the south,' guessed Mike Rowland, 'but there are more shots coming from our side of the river too.'

'Probably a couple of my men,' said Garcia. 'They're doing what I pay them for. They are protecting my land and property from interlopers.'

'Maybe,' answered the Austin deputy, 'but if this carries on then more men are going to get hit and I, for one, have seen enough killing today. Can't you stop them? Seems to me it's your men on this side of the river and it's the settlers on the other side of the water. Listen to those shots. They're not Winchesters. I can hear firing from both sides. If your men kill any of the homesteaders, then I reckon we'll hold you responsible, Garcia. You can't deny this like you denied having anything to do with the raid on the wagons.'

'But they are intruders on my land,' protested Garcia. 'If they weren't trespassing they wouldn't be in danger.'

'So you want them dead, do you?' cut in Marshal Rowland.

'No, I don't, even if they perhaps

deserve it for coming here with dynamite and acting as if they can do whatever they want on my property.'

As he spoke, Garcia spotted something the other three had not seen. At the water's edge a man was desperately clinging to a root growing out of the nearest bank, hanging on so as not to be washed away by what was now a strong flow of water filling the gully which had been the original river channel.

Without hesitation the landowner jumped in and helped the man struggle up the slippery bank. Garcia was in danger of being swept away himself but gradually managed to get the man high enough up the bank for the others to grab his hands and haul him to safety, and then help Garcia up as well. The homesteader was clearly exhausted and appeared to have a deep gash on his forehead.

As he lay recovering, the shooting stopped, and shouting from the other bank came nearer, as his companions tried to locate the man who had been washed downstream in the sudden release of water after they had blown up the rocks which had formed the dam.

By a happy coincidence, the group of homesteaders had decided on direct action on the very occasion that Garcia's property was sparsely guarded because of the attack on the supply wagon. This meant that the Europeans had not been stopped before carrying out their task.

Now six men arrived on the opposite bank from the scene of the river rescue and were relieved to see their companion safely delivered from his ordeal. They were also surprised to see a man in wet Mexican garb seated beside him.

'I am Antonio Garcia,' this man shouted across the water, 'and you men are trespassing on my land. I demand you immediately leave my property and later give your names to the marshal so that you can be charged with trespass. Your companion seems to be recovering but I'm keeping him with me.'

Garcia then turned to the marshal. 'And you three can also leave. You can let me know later what action you intend to take against these trespassers. My father fought a hard battle to win this land and I will not have more interference. Now leave!'

'But what about the man you rescued?' asked Paul Peters.

'I'll get my men to take him back to my *hacienda*, so that he can recover properly. Don't worry. He'll be properly looked after.'

Five days later, however, the man had not reappeared. Marshal Rowland had found out from the other settlers that the homesteader was called Otto Kaufmann, so he decided that he would ride out to his property. There he found his wife in a state of panic. Even though the marshal assured her that her husband was captured but not dead, she refused to be consoled.

'I pleaded with him not to go,' she said. 'How can I manage without him? I am with child and cannot get all the work done by myself. But he insisted he had to go with the others to do something about the dam. Said it was his duty.'

The marshal promised the heavily pregnant woman that he would send help from the town and that he would go to see Garcia the next day. With Luke Granger still deputed to keep Red Roberts locked up, Paul Peters managed to overcome Rowland's resistance when he asked to accompany the marshal.

'You've got no newspaper to report in, so what are you staying for?' asked the lawman. 'Thought you said you were intending to leave Ongar Ridge. This isn't really any of your business. Like you told me, I'm the man wearing the badge. It's my job to find out what Garcia is up to.'

'I know that, but I still haven't found out who killed my uncle. I'd like one more chance to challenge Garcia face to face. It's hard to believe him when he says he knows nothing about the raids on the wagons. And if he does know what his men were up to, then he's as guilty of murder as they are. Seems to me you must be right when you suggest that the stolen goods were eventually finding their way back to his ranch after being hidden somewhere, so I'm still certain he's in league with Trimble. There's no other way his men would know when and where to attack the wagons. If he's guilty of that, then I'm ready to believe he would kill my uncle to protect himself and Trimble.'

'Strange thing, though,' commented Mike Rowland, 'was the way he risked his own life to rescue that settler from drowning in the river. That don't seem like the actions of a killer. But let's see what he's got to say for himself.'

Once again the marshal and Paul Peters were picked up by two of Garcia's men as soon as they rode on to his property. This time their welcome was far from cordial and they were ushered into the *hacienda* under gunpoint.

'What do you want now?' demanded Garcia. 'I've told you to stop coming and bothering me.'

'Quite simply, we want the man you brought here. His wife is pregnant and he needs to get back to her. Surely you don't intend keeping him here as a prisoner? He needs to get back to look after his crops and livestock.'

'And what about *my* crops? He didn't worry about that when he came here with the others to deprive me of water by blowing up my dam.'

'But it's not your river,' cut in Paul Peters. 'You had no right to dam it. The comments in the *Ongar Tribune* were fair. Is that why the editor, Peter Jackson, was killed in his print shop?'

The rancher practically exploded at the direct question. 'How dare you come into my house and accuse me of that. Now get off my land — or else!'

'Or else what?' challenged Marshal Rowland.

'Or else that pregnant woman you spoke about will be missing her husband for quite a while yet. Meanwhile he stays here until I hear he is to hang for shooting one of my men down by the river.'

'That can't be right,' protested the marshal. 'He must have been swept into the river before your men arrived on the scene. How could he have killed one of them?'

'I say he did,' said Garcia, 'and I've got men who will swear that he did. How you going to prove otherwise? Now are you going to leave?'

'Yes, we'll leave, but I insist we take Herr Kaufmann with us. I'm not having him held by you on a ridiculous charge that can't be correct. There's no way he could have killed one of your men when they didn't arrive on the scene until after he'd been washed into the river. He's not guilty of any crime.'

Again Garcia responded to Mike Rowland with a petulant display of anger. 'Not guilty of any crime! You bet he is. He and the others came on to my property in the dead of night with explosives and you say he isn't guilty! They are all guilty and I'm going to make sure they pay for it. So I'm keeping him here. Just you remember to tell his wife that I saved his life. Perhaps I should have let him drown. To tell the truth, I'm not happy at being responsible for him not being present when his wife gives birth, but that's up to you and the other land grabbers who came on to my property. Tell you what I'll do. You get that woman into town to be looked after. I'll pay for her care.'

Again this show of compassion was confusing for his listeners. If Garcia was guilty of organizing, or at least condoning, the deaths of the men on the supply wagons, why was he concerned with the fate of just one of the immigrants he accused of stealing his land? It really didn't add up, and Paul Peters found himself seriously in doubt about the true character of this man.

'How long you thinking of holding Herr Kaufmann?' he asked.

'Until I know the marshal is going to

abide by the law and deal with the trespassers who are making my life so difficult. Now get off my land.'

'OK, we're going,' said the marshal. 'But don't think I am going to let you hold on to the German against his will. That's kidnap in anyone's language,' said the marshal.

16

Back in town, Paul Peters expressed his frustration. 'We can't prove a thing,' he complained to the marshal. 'We can't prove that Garcia ordered the attack on the wagons. We can't prove that he was in league with Trimble. And we certainly can't prove that he had anything to do with my uncle's death.'

Despite his denials, and his show of compassion towards Frau Kaufmann, Garcia still had to be a suspect, if not for committing Peter Jackson's murder himself, then at least for ordering the stabbing in order to cover up whatever the editor knew when he hinted in the newspaper that Garcia was involved in some kind of unspecified conspiracy.

The same applied to Mayor Trimble, who could not be directly connected to any crime. After their return from seeing Garcia, Paul Peters had burst into Trimble's office to confront him, but the mayor had forestalled him. The maps which had previously been pinned to the wall behind him had now disappeared. There could be no way to prove that there was any connection between the number thirty-two shown on the map and the location of the latest attack on the supply wagons.

Once again, Paul Peters had challenged the mayor. 'Did you have anything to do with the death of Peter Jackson?' he asked.

'Absolutely not. And that had better be the last time you accuse me of anything. I'm sick and tired of your insinuations. You're as bad as Peter Jackson was. Now get out of my office.'

* * *

Again Paul Peters departed from a leading suspect with his tail between his legs. Despite his suspicions, he could prove nothing.

Equally, he had no evidence against

the Roberts brothers, much though he considered them thoroughly untrust-worthy and knew that they had worked for both Garcia and Trimble.

Privately, Peters also still considered deputy marshal Luke Granger to be someone who could not be taken at face value. It seemed inherently wrong that the lawman had teamed up with the blacksmith in the beating outside the print shop, even though the marshal had apparently agreed to the deception that Granger was a man who could be bought. From the beginning, Granger had been heard suggesting that the stranger to Ongar Ridge was the man who had killed the editor. Had he been trying to find someone to blame because he was the murderer himself? Had he actually been working for Trimble before he had got the marshal to agree to his double-crossing role?

There were still more questions than answers, but the marshal had a real surprise in store.

★　★　★

When Paul Peters told Marshal Rowland about his further unsuccessful encounter with Trimble, the lawman suddenly asked if he wanted to be sworn in as a deputy so that he could join a small posse he was forming.

'A posse? What's that for? Where are you going, Marshal? Who are you chasing? And what's it got to do with me?'

'I'm not chasing anyone. But I can't let Garcia imprison Otto Kaufmann on his ranch. I'm planning on going in to get him, but I don't fancy I'll be welcome if I go in alone. You've heard Garcia's warnings to keep off his land, so going in with a proper posse is the only way I can do it.'

'Is that legal? Don't you have to get authority?'

'Listen Peters, you're the one who keeps pointing out that I'm the man wearing a badge, so I guess that's all the authority I need. Garcia's breaking the law by holding Kaufmann against his will, so it's my job to do something about it. I've already got a few men from the town, ready for us to go in tomorrow. So do you want to be involved?'

'Count me in, Marshal, even though I was thinking there's no point staying in Ongar Ridge any longer. I'd like to know how things go.'

* ★ *

In all, there were nine in the party which crossed through the entrance arch that marked the boundary into Garcia's land. Unusually they were not at first picked up by Garcia's guards, but their cloud of dust must have been spotted from a distance for they soon saw a horseman racing away towards the *hacienda* to sound a warning of their approach.

Once again, Garcia was waiting on the veranda when they arrived. At first it looked as if he was alone, but as the posse pulled up half a dozen rifles could be seen poking over the balcony which had been used by the young boy with the telescope on their earlier visit. The posse members remained mounted, with their own weapons at the ready.

'So, Marshal, you've chosen again to ignore my warnings,' called Garcia in a carefully controlled voice. 'What do you mean by coming here in force? What do you want?'

'I'm sure you can guess, Garcia. We want Kaufmann. I aim to take him back with me. As you can see, there's enough of us to make sure you hand him over. And, what's more, I want you to come, too, so that you can answer questions about the raids on the supply wagons.'

'Marshal, I think you've miscalculated. You've possibly got enough guns to shoot your way in and get the German, though you'll have to kill me first. But what's more significant is that you'll be responsible for the deaths of some of these men you've got with you. You can no doubt see the rifles pointing down at you. Any move forward by you, and bullets will rain down on you from my balcony. How will you explain away the deaths of these good townsfolk — even if you remain alive yourself to do any explaining to the wives and other kin of the men you have brought out here? You haven't even got a good reason for being here. All I'm guilty of is looking after the health of a man who isn't well enough to ride after nearly drowning. I'm just being a charitable neighbour, doing the poor man a favour after rescuing him myself. He owes me his life, so I can't see him ever complaining about being invited to rest up a while in very comfortable sur-roundings. So, Marshal, I suggest you just turn around and go back to town. And I'm certainly not coming with you, so you can forget that.'

Marshal Rowland had listened with-out interruption whilst Garcia delivered his mildly spoken response, but he was aware of muttering behind him as some of the posse members accepted the reality that any further action would probably result in some of them not staying alive. Despite their superior numbers, they were the ones most vulnerable if shooting started. This was acknowledged by a man the marshal knew to be the father of three children.

'Guess he's right, Marshal,' said this man. 'We stand to be the losers.'

Marshal Rowland recognized that Garcia had bested him. He had gained nothing by coming in with a posse, since there was no way he could justify risking the lives of the men who had accompanied him. He tried one last ploy.

'Garcia, you say you are simply nursing Kaufmann back to health, rather than holding him as a hostage. If that's true, I guess you won't object to one of his friends coming in, unarmed, to tell him his wife has given birth to a bouncing baby boy.'

'Nice try, Rowland, but it won't work. No one's coming in past me, whether armed or not. But don't you worry, Marshal, I'll pass the message on. Now I'll be obliged if you'll get out of here.'

Reluctantly, the marshal accepted the inevitable and turned to order the posse members to ride out. His face, though, reflected his inner rage.

17

On the ride back, a couple of farmers peeled away from the posse to return to their respective homes, but they left with hardly a word spoken to the marshal. The general feeling of frustration, resentment and anger was palpable, and when the small remaining group reached the town, a respected early settler demanded to know what action their lawman intended to take.

'Garcia is running rings around us,' claimed the spokesman. 'First he dams the river, and then he captures Kaufmann when we decide to do something about it. We're all wary of what he might do next. We know that other cattlemen have been taking direct action against settlers, and we're all scared of what might happen here in reprisal for us blowing up the dam. What are you going to do about it, Marshal?'

'Listen, men, I'm as fed up as you. I'm sorry we've all had a wasted day, but there was no way I could risk some of you being killed out at the ranch. I'll get Kaufmann back somehow. I promise you that, but I want all of you to remain vigilant. Personally, I don't expect Garcia to take any direct action against you. He's not done anything against any of the settlers, except to stop more newcomers encroaching on to what he sees as his rightful territory, and I don't expect him to do anything more now, so let's just stay wary and rely on the authorities in Austin to deal with the matter of the raids on the wagons. That, after all, involves murder, so you can't say nothing is being done. Now let's all go home and I'll keep you informed.'

★　★　★

The marshal's defensive speech did little to quell the general feeling of dissatisfaction, but the remaining few members of the aborted posse did disperse, albeit with a deal of murmurings expressing the worries felt by the whole community.

Angry at his own failure to return Kaufmann to his wife and newly born son, Marshal Rowland also had to acknowledge that he was losing the support he had been accustomed to receiving from the citizens of Ongar Ridge and the surrounding area.

'I've got to do something to shake Garcia out of his dominant position,' he said when he joined Mrs Pullman, Jessica Shackleton and Paul Peters for an evening meal. 'I plan to go in alone at night, locate Kaufmann and get him out.'

'Sounds like an act of desperation to me. You'd never come out alive and that won't do anyone a favour,' commented Bessie Pullman.

'Got any better ideas?' spat out the lawman.

Surprisingly, the usually reserved Jessica was the one who spoke up.

'What about a prisoner exchange? The sheriff in Austin has got several of Garcia's men under arrest and I bet Garcia would like them back. Couldn't one of them be offered in exchange for Herr Kaufmann?'

Mike Rowland turned the idea over in his mind, but then decided it was probably not possible. 'I can't see the sheriff releasing anyone who he thinks might be guilty of murdering those people in the supply wagons.'

Paul Peters then cut in. 'OK. But how about someone nearer to home? Why can't we keep Red Roberts in jail and send his brother in to Garcia to try to negotiate an exchange? We know both brothers worked for Garcia, so maybe he would agree. After all, there's no real reason for him to hold on to Kaufmann, and he knows we won't stop trying different tactics after our posse didn't succeed. It's worth a try.'

* * *

Getting Ned Roberts to agree to the plan was not so easy, however. He first protested that the marshal had no right to hold Red in jail, and had absolutely no authority to use him as the centre of a bargaining ploy. 'Anyway, why should I risk my life riding in there? Garcia is just as likely to keep me, or even kill me, as he is to release this German. All Red and me ever did was run a few messages to Garcia, so I don't suppose he'll be too bothered to hear that you've got my brother locked up.'

The marshal tried a different approach. 'What if I said there would be a cash reward for anyone who can help rescue the German?'

The offer of payment apparently appealed more to Ned Roberts than the aim of getting his brother released. After a little negotiation over the amount, he agreed to try the suggested gambit — though he would not have been so keen if he had realized that the marshal had no authority to offer a reward, but was not concerned at tricking one of the troublesome Roberts brothers. In the event the lawman's deceit was not tested because Ned's mission proved to be fruitless. He rode out early the next morning but returned empty-handed a few hours later.

'Garcia says no deal!' he reported back. 'But you better let my brother free anyway. You've no right to hold him. He ain't done anything.'

* * *

Still frustrated at his lack of success, Mike Rowland was to suffer a further blow to his morale when Mayor Trimble sent a message to say that he was going to call a town council meeting at which he would propose that the marshal be dismissed, and he would then hold a public meeting in the town square.

By six o'clock in the evening a reasonable crowd had gathered by the time Trimble arrived and climbed up onto a platform to address his audience.

'Thank you for coming, my dear neighbours,' he started in his usual unctuous tone.

Immediately one of the homesteaders reacted. 'Don't call us neighbours,' he shouted. 'You ain't no friend of ours. You're bleeding us dry with the prices you charge us.'

Trimble cleverly used the attack as an opportunity to make his pitch. 'I know you're suffering, folks, but so am I. You'll all know that another supply train has been attacked and that means we are short of essential goods. It's hurting us all — you and me. Believe me when I tell you that I have no choice but to increase some of my prices and charge interest to those who owe me money.'

Again a heckler interrupted. 'At least you've got money,' he shouted. 'Many of us ain't got a thing.'

'I know things are tough,' countered the mayor, 'and I'll tell you why if you'll just listen to me . . . '

He was interrupted, however, by a surprise arrival. To everyone's delight, Otto Kaufmann rode into town. He was soon surrounded by well-wishers anxious to find out what had happened.

'Did you escape?' 'How did you get away?' 'How did you get your horse?' 'Are you OK?'

The questions came thick and fast, but Kaufmann again surprised everyone by jumping up on to the stage and saying that, after Ned Roberts was sent away empty-handed, the sheriff had arrived from Austin with a large posse. 'Garcia's been arrested,' he told the excited crowd. 'Apparently some of the men who raided the supply wagons have admitted that Garcia had arranged the whole thing, and the earlier raids as well. The sheriff has taken him back to Austin for questioning to find out how Garcia knew where to attack.'

As the crowd absorbed this news, Marshal Rowland fired a shot into the air to quieten the noisy gathering. He, in turn, mounted the makeshift stage. 'Listen folks,' he shouted. As the crowd quietened, he caught their absolute attention by turning his Colt towards Trimble. 'I've got things to tell you about your mayor,' he said. 'He called this meeting to try to get you to vote me out of office. His reason? It's simple. He wants me out of the way because Paul Peters here — the man some of you still think killed our editor — has discovered the truth. The rogue who tipped off Garcia is this man here — the man I am now going to arrest. The same man who has been making you pay over the odds for your essentials. The man from Chicago who has got rich at your expense. It's Eustace Trimble who told Garcia when the supplies meant for you could be taken by force. He's going to jail, folks.'

The marshal's revelation got a mixed reaction he hadn't really expected. Some cheered; some jeered; then some began pushing forward in anger, threatening to attack the man they had voted in as mayor but now wanted brought to justice.

Suddenly the angry mood escalated. Encouraged by shouts calling for action, the whole crowd surged forward. Trimble was pushed backwards from the stage and surrounded by a whole group who shoved him against a wall and started pummelling him.

Surprised by the sudden determination of the group, Marshall Rowland was left behind by the surge of angry men. From his position on the stage, he was powerless to intervene. With his Colt still in his hand, he fired three more shots into the air. 'Stop this,' he shouted. 'Let's do this legally. The days of lynching are behind us. Let me deal with it.'

His voice was drowned out by the general hubbub, however, and his pleas were ignored. As he tried to push his way through the crowd towards where Mayor Trimble was being attacked, he heard someone shout 'He's finished!'.

Quickly and silently those gathered

around Trimble backed away and dispersed, leaving the marshal able to see the mayor's body on the ground. It didn't take much of an examination to see that the man was indeed dead. He had been strangled, as well as being punched and kicked, though it was impossible to know which of the crowd had actually dealt the final punishing act.

18

With no newspaper to run, Trimble killed by unknown hands, and Kaufmann safely returned, Paul Peters found himself with too much idle time on his hands.

Despite his protests, Bessie Pullman had stopped charging him for his lodgings, though he continued to pay her for food.

He repaid her to some extent by carrying out minor household repairs which had accumulated since her husband's death. He also tidied up and planted the little bit of land around her house, and even gave her some unskilled assistance in the bakery.

He had just about given up all hope of finding out anything new relating to his uncle's death, and was now resolved to leaving Ongar Ridge. And there was also a further incident involving the blacksmith, Shackleton, to make Peters aware that his stay in the town was not universally welcomed. His newspaper campaigning had been respected by many, but there were a good number of people who still suspected that the newcomer might be the man who had murdered Peter Jackson.

The two Roberts brothers were still vocal in their accusations, and so was Shackleton. The blacksmith clearly carried a deep-rooted grudge against Paul Peters. He couldn't forget the treatment he had received when he had stormed into Bessie Pullman's house to reclaim his wife after she had fled from his ill treatment. Now she was still living with the widow, and Shackleton built up his suspicions that being under the same roof as Peters might be part of the reason for her refusal to return to the marital home.

The hatred came to a head when Shackleton saw Paul Peters escorting Jessica to buy provisions.

They were passing the rear of the

smithy when Shackleton confronted them. He was brandishing a length of metal that was still red from the heat of the forge's furnace. He advanced towards the couple with an unsteady gait, suggesting that he was perhaps still under the influence of alcohol, even though it was mid-morning. 'What you doing with my woman?' he demanded in a slurred voice.

Jessica spoke up first. 'He's just walking alongside me. Don't make anything of it, William.'

'What you mean, don't make anything of it? You've deserted me, and now I see you with this murderer! I'm gonna finish him.'

Jessica and Paul Peters backed away as Shackleton advanced, holding the hot metal rod aloft. Already a few observers had stopped to watch the scene.

Worried by the determined expression on Shackleton's face, Paul Peters tried to calm the man as he encouraged Jessica to move further away from her estranged husband.

'Don't be stupid, man,' he counselled. 'You'll be in real trouble if you harm either of us with that thing.'

The warning went unheeded, however, as Shackleton continued to advance with his improvised weapon held high. 'Both of you deserve a bit of punishment.' He swung the hot rod in an arc but staggered as he did so, giving Paul Peters a chance to step in and aim a hefty kick at the blacksmith's leg.

The blow was enough to throw Shackleton completely off balance. He stumbled for three unsteady steps before falling to the ground with his arm coming to rest on the hot metal. The poor man screamed in pain before Peters pulled him away and put out the burning clothing that was searing his flesh. Bystanders came to help, whilst one ran off to get the doctor. It was clear that quick action from Paul Peters had limited the damage that had been done to his assailant's arm, but it was likely that it would be some time before the blacksmith would be able to continue his trade.

Although Shackleton's injury was of his own making, there was little doubt that his twisted sense of justice would mean that he would hold Peters responsible. The threat of future retaliatory action was impossible for Paul Peters to ignore, and added to his increasing determination to return east.

What was really surprising, however, was Jessica's reaction to the incident. When her husband had fallen to the ground she had rushed over to help beat out the flames on his clothing. She was weeping and had to be comforted by one of the townswomen, whilst they waited for the doctor to arrive.

When Shackleton had been treated and returned home, Jessica had gathered her things from Bessie Pullman's and moved back in with him, so that she could act as his nurse. The widow and others had tried to dissuade her, but she had been insistent that it was her duty as his wife. 'I have to do it,' she said. 'And I don't think he'll treat me so badly again if I look after him in his time of need.'

A further factor was that, whilst his arm was healing, Shackleton could not continue to earn a living. He managed to persuade one of the other town residents to undertake the most urgent work, but it was not long before the blacksmith returned to his old gambling and drinking habits, whilst Jessica managed to support them with the meagre wages she got from working in the bakery. It was an arrangement which surprised everyone who knew the history of their marriage, and there was considerable admiration for the young woman's dedication to her wedding vows.

19

Paul Peters was in the Golden Bullet one wet evening, taking his time over what he had decided would be his last beer in Ongar Ridge, as he had now definitely made up his mind to leave Texas and return to Virginia, having failed to identify his uncle's killer.

Visiting the saloon was something he had got into the habit of doing once or twice a week — not because he was interested in gambling or even the general atmosphere, but he had sometimes been able to pick up useful bits of local information which he could legitimately include in the *New Tribune* when it was still being published.

For his final visit he had stayed later than usual, as much as anything because he was sheltering from heavy rain, rather than walking back to his lodgings at Bessie Pullman's house. He had been chatting for some while to a couple of homesteaders who were complaining about the extremely hot and dry weather they had been suffering from, with today's torrential rain now going to the other extreme. 'Hope it doesn't keep going too long,' one of the farmers was saying, 'though the weather's not so important now that we don't have to worry too much about losing the water from the river Garcia blocked up.'

Still interested in the farmers' feud with Garcia, Peters asked what the homesteaders thought would happen in the longer run, but his question was not heard because of the increasing level of noise from raised voices coming from a group of card players at a large nearby table. 'Can't hear you,' the farmer had to shout, 'and, anyway, reckon I better be getting back whether or not it's still pouring. The row is from that usual drunken lot, including the two Roberts brothers again. Think there might be trouble brewing if the cards don't go their way. Think I'll alert the marshal on my way home.'

Mike Rowland appeared less than five minutes later, accompanied by his deputy, Luke Granger. They were just in time to hear Red Roberts accuse fellow card player Butch Woods of cheating.

'Damn you, Roberts. You just don't know how to lose with dignity,' claimed his opponent as he threw his cards on the table and started to rise from his chair. He didn't fully get to his feet, however, because he was shot in the chest by Red's brother Ned. The man slumped forward on to the table, and immediately pandemonium broke out in the saloon, with all the customers seeking to scramble away from the incident.

Standing at the bar, Luke Granger was quick to respond. 'Drop that weapon, Ned,' he ordered, but perhaps instinctively, Roberts fired again. One bullet smashed harmlessly into the saloon's woodwork, but the second hit the deputy in the throat. Speedily, Marshal Rowland had moved to one side. He deliberately fired into the ceiling to indicate his readiness to shoot, and issued his own instruction. 'Nobody move,' he shouted. 'And you toss that Colt away, Roberts.'

But once again, Ned ignored the command. He turned to face the marshal, who didn't hesitate. He pulled the trigger and dropped the second of the Roberts brothers to die at his hand. It was a point not lost on Red, who had dived for shelter behind the table that had been used for the disputed card game.

'You bastard, Rowland,' he shouted. 'First Jed, now Ned. Well you ain't gonna get me!'

He upturned the table and using it as a shield, fired at the marshal. The bullet caught Mike Rowland in the shoulder and he dropped to the floor, losing his revolver in the process.

Roberts immediately rose from behind the table and quickly moved over to where the marshal had fallen. He glared down at the lawman. 'I'm gonna drill you full of holes, you rotten bastard,' he snarled as he fired two more shots — one at each of the marshal's legs. He raised his sight a little, ready for another shot, but Paul Peters beat him to it. There was a look of disbelief on Red's face as the Virginian's bullet entered his body just below the heart. Slowly his legs buckled and he toppled forward to fall on top of the marshal.

The onlookers needed a few moments to register what had happened, then those who had stood back in safety moved forward to examine the carnage. It didn't take long to establish that there were four dead — the unlucky card player Butch Woods, Ned and Red Roberts, and deputy marshal Luke Granger.

Mike Rowland was still alive, having taken three bullets in non-vital areas. As Paul Peters pulled the dead Red Roberts to one side, the marshal displayed a macabre sense of humour. 'Guess that makes you and me about even, but it's a pity your newspaper's gone. You'd have had plenty to write about this week,' he whispered before falling unconscious.

*   *   *

Although relieved at the marshal's survival, Paul Peters was dismayed that this incident had made him kill a man — and which also seemed to confirm that he now had no chance at all of establishing the identity of his uncle's killer.

Despite any supporting evidence, the Roberts brothers and Luke Granger had all remained as possible suspects. Now they were all dead. So, too, was Trimble.

Paul Peters had accepted that he would never solve the mystery, when he suddenly remembered an earlier conversation he had had with Jake Thornton, which he had paid little attention to at the time.

'Mr Peters,' the youngster had asked after they had finalized the first issue of the New Tribune. 'Aren't you going to post bill-boards like Mr Jackson did?'

'What do you mean?'

'Well, every Friday evening he used to print off some single sheets saying what the main story would be in the week's newspaper. Then we used to go round pinning them up in lots of places to get people talking and buying the paper.'

Paul Peters recalled what he had heard at his own trial. 'Did he usually display a poster outside the newspaper office itself?'

'Sure did! That was always the first to go up.'

'But can you remember, Jake, if he did one the night before he died?'

'No, he didn't. I thought it was strange he didn't give us any to take round the town, but the first thing I saw when I arrived the next morning was

208

the one outside with just the one word on it.'

* * *

Now, as he watched the doctor deal with the injuries to the marshal in the Golden Bullet, Peters started to explore in his mind possible explanations for the unusual behaviour Jake had mentioned earlier. His thoughts also began to question again the details of his uncle's stabbing. He had always assumed that the knife had been used, rather than a revolver, in order to commit a silent murder. But perhaps there was another explanation.

The next day he went back to talk to the undertaker, Jasper Ryan. The man was busy preparing the four bodies for their burial when he remarked that it was easier than his work on Peter Jackson, with the gaping knife wound to be dealt with.

Peters' thoughts jerked back to what

he had heard in court about the editor's death.

'What happened to the knife used to kill Peter Jackson?' he asked the undertaker.

The man had no hesitation. 'After the doctor had examined him I withdrew it from his stomach and cleaned it up. Strange thing was that there was ink inside the wound, not just poured over his body. I think the ink might have been on him before the knife went in. Didn't know who to give the Bowie to until Bessie Pullman came round the next day. She said she would pay my charges. Said she held some money that belonged to the dead man, so I took up her offer. Didn't seem too funny that she held some of his money, since I know he lodged with her.'

'And the knife?'

'She asked for it. Said it had belonged to Mr Jackson, and she wanted to keep it as a kind of memento. Perhaps I shouldn't say this, but we all thought the relationship between those two was a bit more than just a business arrangement, so I was happy to let her have it. There was no need for me to sell any of his things, as she was paying my bill.'

Peters pressed the point. 'And she definitely said the knife belonged to Peter Jackson?'

'Yes, that's right. It had a most distinctive pattern on the handle. Couldn't be a mistake. Mrs Pullman swore it was his.'

'And she took it away?'

'Yep. Why do you ask? Is it important, Mr Peters?'

'Could be.' Paul Peters said no more, but wasted no time before he tackled Bessie Pullman about it.

* * *

'I'm told you've got the knife that was pulled out of the editor's body. Is that correct?' he asked her that evening.

She went red, in a sign of embarrassment, and hesitated before answering.

'How did you know that?' she countered.

'The undertaker told me, but I want to know the significance behind it. Why did you want it? What does it mean to you? Did you have something to do with Peter Jackson's murder? Were *you* the one who stuck the knife into him?'

The questions came out in a torrent as, for the first time, Paul Peters considered the possibility that this woman was actually the killer he had been seeking to uncover. Who knew what disagreements or ill feeling might have developed between these two who had lived under the same roof for a considerable period of time? If she had a motive, she certainly also had the knowledge and opportunity to have gone to the newspaper premises and stabbed the editor, who — unsuspecting — would not have resisted an approach from this woman he knew so well. Following this new chain of thought, Peters continued his questions.

'How did the knife get to the print shop? Did my uncle usually carry it with him? Or did you take it as the intended weapon? Did you kill him?'

Instead of answering, Bessie Pullman picked up on one significant word in the questions.

'Your *uncle*?' she asked. 'Peter was your *uncle*? You didn't tell me that before. Why did you keep it a secret? Does anyone else know? Is that why you came to Ongar Ridge?'

20

After the heated exchange of questions and answers, Peters and Bessie Pullman sat and had a long discussion. He explained about the letter his mother had received, revealing something of his uncle's disappearance, and his remorse at some incident that was probably associated with what had taken place during the war between the north and south.

He described to her his own decision to travel west, and how, in San Antonio, he had spotted the likely link between his uncle's real name of Jack Peters and the inversion to 'Peter Jackson'. He recalled his extreme bad luck at arriving on the evening before his uncle's death. 'If I had made contact with him immediately I arrived, I'm sure he would still be alive today.'

'But the date of his death wasn't

random,' said the widow. 'Every year the beginning of July was always his lowest point. Every year he's been here he has gone into a fit of despondency at that time — and this year it was even worse.'

Mrs Pullman stopped in her narrative and seemed to be near to tears, obviously distressed as she recalled the incident of a few weeks ago. 'To answer your question, I didn't kill him, and neither did anyone else. I'm sure of that.'

'Go on,' urged her attentive listener, unsure what she was suggesting.

Still obviously upset, Bessie Pullman described how, before setting off to her bakery that morning, she had checked on her lodger's room. She was later than usual because she knew Jessica Shackleton was scheduled to open up and get things started in the bakery. As she expected, she saw from his empty room that Peter Jackson had left before dawn to go to the newspaper premises — but she had immediately noticed that the Bowie knife was not in its usual place beside his wash bowl.

'He always left it there,' she said. 'He never carried a weapon of any kind, and I had never known him to take the knife from its usual place. As soon as I saw it was gone I knew something was wrong.'

Again she hesitated. Although anxious to hear the rest of her story, Paul Peters remained silent whilst she recovered her composure.

'I heard noise over at the print shop,' she eventually continued. 'When I checked, I found a small crowd had gathered. Then Marshal Rowland came out to say that poor Peter had been killed. But I knew what had happened as soon as I saw the JUSTICE notice outside. I was certain that the remorse he had carried with him for so many years had finally become too much to live with. I knew he had killed himself. He posted the notice himself and then went inside. I'm sure he poured the ink on himself and then stabbed himself with the second notice already pierced on the knife blade.'

Bessie Pullman stopped her flow of words, wiped tears from her eyes, and then continued. 'When I heard the details at your trial I knew exactly what had happened. Peter took the knife to the print shop with the intention of killing himself as some kind of penance. That's what the JUSTICE notices were all about. Speak to Jessica if you want confirmation. She'll tell you that, on her way to the bakery premises early that morning, she saw Peter pinning a notice outside the print shop. She couldn't see exactly what it said, but she is sure it was just one word. We know now that word was 'JUSTICE'. Believe me, no one else was to blame for his killing. He did it himself.'

Paul Peters cut in, 'Yet you let me go on trial for his murder! I could have finished up at the end of a rope!'

'No, it wouldn't have been like that. Because I was certain what had happened, I knew there couldn't be any real evidence against you. I was ready to speak up if necessary, but there was no need when Judge Kane stopped your trial. Believe me, your uncle was basically a good man and I didn't want the town's memory of him to be a bad one. Suicide is something of a dirty word in these parts. The past has gone to his grave with him and I wanted his death to remain as an unsolved mystery. That's why I kept silent.'

'And what about me?' persisted the man who had been accused of the killing.

'I thought you would ride away once you were freed. Didn't expect you to stay, but then I didn't know anything about your connection to your uncle. And now that I do know your relationship, I think I should tell you what he blurted out to me the night before he died. I was bold enough to ask him why he was always in such a state at the same time every year.'

She paused, then continued the explanation. 'Apparently it is the anniversary of Gettysburg, and that is when it happened.'

'What happened? What caused him so much pain every year?'

Sobbing now, Bessie Pullman almost choked on her words. 'He killed his brother. Your uncle told me that he killed your father!'

'What? That can't be right. My mother always told me they were very close. Why would he have killed my pa?' demanded her shattered listener.

'It was a mercy killing. Your father was badly injured and in terrible pain. He begged your uncle to end it before the Union soldiers made it to where they were hiding in a ditch after two of them had pulled your father away from the cavalry battle. Out of compassion, Peter killed his brother, and that is the crime he has lived with for all these years. He did it with the same knife that he used to kill himself. That must have been why he kept it always in sight in his room for all those years. He poured out the whole story to me, using me as some kind of confessional listener. I don't know why he didn't go to the priest.'

Seeming anxious to remember all of what she had been told the night before the suicide, Bessie Pullman recalled her lodger saying that initially he never really wanted to join the war. He felt he had little in common with the wealthy plantation owners who were desperate to defend their right to buy and own slaves. As small-time farmers and horse breeders, the two Peters brothers were well aware of the financial power of cotton and knew that the family business inherited from their dead father indirectly depended on the sweat of the black men whose labours underpinned the economy of the Southern states. After the Southerners' attack on Fort Sumter in April 1861, they listened to the heated debates in the Virginian saloon they visited occasionally and gradually found themselves building a growing conviction that the Yankees did not have a right to impose their values on their southern neighbours. Who were they to dictate that the south should be forced to end their reliance on slave-owning?

Most importantly, the brothers came to regard their loyalty to Virginia as paramount. Secession from the Union seemed to be justified against the northern bigots' pressures. And so it was that Jack Peters and his brother Bruce reluctantly left Laura and her son Peter to wave goodbye to them when they rode off with a small band of neighbours to join the growing forces being established to counter the northern army. They were all persuaded that the fighting would be short-lived and they would soon be back home.

'How wrong we were,' a distraught Jack Peters had told Bessie Pullman, before relating the story of the mercy killing he had decided he could no longer keep on his conscience. He said he had been sickened by the whole business of war and had simply deserted, travelling all the way out to

Texas, believing that he could not return safely to his home area, where at least one companion knew his story.

Wondering how Paul Peters was going to react to her shocking revelation of the history behind his uncle's suicide, Bessie Pullman again wiped tears from her eyes and turned to the young man. 'What are you going to do now you know the truth?' she asked. 'You do believe me, don't you?'

Paul Peters hesitated for only a few moments. 'Yes, I believe you. It all adds up. And I guess you're right about leaving the story as an unresolved mystery. Let everyone continue to think it was a murder, even though you've convinced me that it wasn't. No point in spoiling my uncle's reputation. Marshal Rowland will get help to sort out the business of the bandit raids on the supply wagons, so there's no need for me to be involved in that. Think I'll be riding out in the morning now I know there's no murderer for me to uncover. No point me staying here.'

Bessie Pullman had the last word. In a flat, emotionless voice she simply said 'Shame,' without any further explanation to reveal her thoughts.

Epilogue

Paul Peters had no regrets about leaving Ongar Ridge and returning to Virginia. After his mother had died, he had left the east on something of a whim, taking with him the letter she had received from her brother-in-law.

He had known before that his own father, Bruce Peters, had died at Gettysburg but his uncle Jack had been officially simply listed as missing. However, the letter sent from Texas had made it clear that Paul's only remaining relative had somehow survived the slaughter that had, in total, claimed the lives of over six hundred thousand men.

During the war, Paul's mother Laura had struggled to keep the two of them alive. Combatants in both grey and blue uniforms had confiscated their horses and had helped themselves to vegetables from their small area of cultivated land. Unlike many other properties, their house had been left untouched and Laura had helped them survive by taking on whatever odd jobs she could for neighbouring wives whose husbands had gone off to fight.

After the hostilities finally ended, young Paul studied hard, but then had no real idea what to do with his life until his mother's death had served as the catalyst which made him decide to undertake the probably hopeless task of tracking down his uncle.

With Bessie Pullman's revelations in Ongar Ridge he had succeeded in solving the mystery of his uncle's death, but still decided to keep silent about the relationship between them.

Bessie Pullman seemed relieved to have been able to relay to Paul Peters the horror story that had been told to her by the dead man, but was concerned that this should remain confidential. The two of them vowed to keep the suicide as a secret, and maintain the fiction of a mystery dawn death in the print shop.

They were aware that, despite the deaths of the Roberts brothers, there were still some people in the town who retained the suspicion that it could not be a coincidence that Paul Peters had arrived in Ongar Ridge the same night that the editor died. Some regarded Judge Kane's dismissal of the murder charge as somewhat facile, even though there was patently no evidence that could be levelled at the newcomer.

Even some of those who accepted the positive role Paul Peters had played in revealing the mayor's crooked set-up still considered it was possible that the young newcomer had somehow been responsible for the death of the respected editor.

It was against this background that Paul Peters decided to travel back east, where he still had some possessions in the care of his Virginian neighbour.

He decided, however, that he would travel back by first returning to San Antonio. He had a natural curiosity to visit the historic Alamo, where the small group of many nationalities had given their lives to resist Santa Anna.

His initial task, though, was to visit the *San Antonio Express* editor who had first made him aware of the existence of 'Peter Jackson' in the nearby town of Ongar Ridge. Still without revealing his relationship to the dead man, Paul Peters provided more details of the events that had taken place there.

'I've already printed most of it,' the newsman said. 'For a small town you've had quite a run of interesting stories. It's not often an editor gets stabbed to death and a mayor gets strangled by an angry mob — not to mention other shootings. And we're still covering the story about the ambushing of supply wagons. I understand you had something to do with that?'

'Yes,' acknowledged his visitor, 'but all the credit must go to the marshal.'

'The one who got shot in a saloon shoot-out? How's he progressing now?'

'Recovering well, according to the doc — though he's always going to walk with a limp.'

'And what about you?' asked the editor.

'Me? I'm heading back to Virginia.'

'And you're going back without telling me why the devil you came here in the first place?'

Paul Peters smiled. 'Let's just say I wanted an adventure. I'll call it my Texan adventure . . .'

Once back in Virginia, he set about rebuilding his life. The Texas adventure, as he called it, seemed to have effectively been brought to a conclusion with a letter from the Ongar Ridge lawyer, Charles Fisher, dated 4 August 1881:

Dear Paul,
Thank you for the letter you left for me with Bessie Pullman. I'm sorry I didn't get to say farewell.

You'll perhaps not be surprised to learn that it is now common

228

knowledge that the man we knew as Peter Jackson was actually your uncle Jack. The word soon spread once you had revealed the truth to Mrs Pullman. She couldn't keep that secret, though I think she did it for the right motives. She wanted people to understand why you had become so involved in the business of our editor's untimely death. Without giving more details, she told her customers that she is certain you were not guilty of his murder, so it has stayed as a mystery that will never be solved.

(I am returning the letter your uncle wrote to your mother as proof of your connection to him, and the bank readily accepted affidavits from Mike Rowland and myself that you were entitled to the little money he had built up during his time with us. But as you requested, I arranged for the money left in your uncle's account to be passed to Mrs Pullman.)

You'll be interested to know that the authorities have at last made progress with action against Garcia. It seems that they didn't know exactly what crimes to charge him with, since he personally didn't do physical harm to anyone. Initially, some of his men jailed in Austin refused to make specific accusations against their boss, but when they found themselves accused of murdering the guards on the supply wagons they changed their evidence and said they were acting under his orders. Although they are all guilty as a group, no one can actually prove who fired the shots and it just dragged on while there were accusations, counter accusations and denials. And, of course, Trimble was not around to be involved. As a lawyer myself, I think it sounds like a legal mess, but the latest news is that it is clear that Garcia cannot escape the body of evidence that has built up around him. I think the least he can expect is a very long time in jail, even if he escapes the rope around his neck.

No one has ever been accused of Trimble's murder, with it not even being clear who in the crowd was closest to him when he was strangled. An effective wall of silence built up around that incident. No one claimed a right to his business and it's now being run by two men from the town on much fairer terms, so most of the homesteaders are getting on much better now that they are clear of their debts.

Finally — a bit of surprising personal news. The day after you left, blacksmith William Shackleton was shoeing a horse whilst in a hung-over state when the animal decided to kick him in the head. Shackleton had some form of seizure and died that night. Now, apparently, Marshal Rowland has been seeing quite a bit of the young widow, Jessica, and the gossipy Bessie Pullman has even been hinting at a wedding in the offing. We had all got the marshal down as a loner who was not really interested in women, but we were clearly wrong. You ought to know that he's become quite a celebrity. He fully acknowledged your valuable part in making the connection between Trimble's messages to Garcia and the raids, but he is personally getting all the credit for tracking down the bandits and their capture by the sheriff. The San Antonio newspaper has written a couple of glowing reports about what he did and described him as 'The Hopalong Marshal', on account of the injuries to his legs. In fact Mike Rowland is now regarded as our local hero.

He has got himself a competent young deputy and there is talk that the marshal might stand for election as our town mayor.

Some of us had thought you might stay in Ongar Ridge, and perhaps even open a newspaper again. However, I do understand your realization that there are still a few people around who think it is possible that you killed your uncle — perhaps as some sort of family feud or vendetta. Bessie Pullman has been vociferous in shouting down any suggestions of that kind but his untimely death has remained a public mystery.

Anyway, I personally fully understand your decision to return to Virginia, and trust you are able to successfully rebuild your life there.

Yours, Charles Fisher

We do hope that you have enjoyed reading this large print book.

Did you know that all of our titles are available for purchase?

We publish a wide range of high quality large print books including:
Romances, Mysteries, Classics
General Fiction
Non Fiction and Westerns

Special interest titles available in large print are:
The Little Oxford Dictionary
Music Book, Song Book
Hymn Book, Service Book

Also available from us courtesy of Oxford University Press:
Young Readers' Dictionary
(large print edition)
Young Readers' Thesaurus
(large print edition)

For further information or a free brochure, please contact us at:
Ulverscroft Large Print Books Ltd.,
The Green, Bradgate Road, Anstey,
Leicester, LE7 7FU, England.
Tel: (00 44) **0116 236 4325**
Fax: (00 44) **0116 234 0205**